LET THE WATERS ROAR

Geonn Cannon

Supposed Crimes LLC • Matthews, North Carolina

This book is a work of fiction. Names, characters, places, and incidents are products of the author's imagination or are used fictitiously. Any resemblance to actual events or locales or persons, living or dead, is entirely coincidental.

www.supposedcrimes.com

This book is typeset in Goudy Old Style.

LET THE WATERS ROAR

PROLOGUE

Islas Baleares
Before everything

"OFTENTIMES HAVE *we laid out, toil nor danger fearing,*" the men sang. "*Tugging out the flapping sail to the weather hearing...*"

The sound of men singing followed Harriet Landau from the tavern. She craved the reverie of their company, the drink and companionship that proved she had finally been accepted as one of the crew. But she couldn't waste time with them tonight. She had a mission. Their song echoed off the trees ringing the beach and could still be heard on the stone footpath that led deeper into the jungle. Harriet hummed along, muttering the words under her breath as she ventured farther from the safety of civilization.

The path grew darker with each step, but she wouldn't allow herself to turn back now. She had been instructed not to bring a lantern, but she hadn't expected just how fully dark it would be. The moonlight barely penetrated the ceiling of foliage above her head. She had to take great care not to trip or turn her ankle, grateful for the flintlock on one hip and the cutlass on the other should anyone attempt to follow her.

As frightening as it was to forge ahead, she refused to turn back. She could accept failure or disappointment, but she would not abide surrender. So she continued blindly, trusting the information she'd been given was accurate.

Before long, she was far enough from the cavern that the singing was no longer audible. She was too deep into the forest to see any moonlight. She swept the ground in front of her with the toe of her boot before taking a step, her arms extended to explore the space ahead of her for any branches or trees she needed to avoid. Her heart thrummed hard against her ribs as she tried very hard not to think about how she would find her way back to the beach.

A hand closed around her wrist.

Despite telling herself to be brave, she yelped and tried to pull away. The initial surge of panic was strong enough that she didn't reach for any of her weapons, a fact which may have saved her life.

"Don't fight, don't fret." The voice sounded like a crow cawing from the darkness. "It's nothing but what you came for, innit? Finally get where you're going and try to run away? No smarts in that!" The woman cackled and pulled on Harriet's arm. "Here we go, lass, a bit more bright just around the corner here, you can bet on it."

Harriet allowed herself to be escorted around a corner she couldn't see. As promised, she was suddenly surrounded by a glow so bright that it stabbed her eyes. She brought up her free hand to block it, crying out in pain and surprise. The old woman released her hand, cackling at her reaction. Harriet rubbed at her eyes and finally risked opening them again. She squinted at her new surroundings.

She was in a squat wooden structure with a table, two chairs, a sea of pillows on the ground, and bottles lined up on boxes that were stacked on crates that all leaned precariously against each other. The walls seemed to be slapped together with a tacky golden substance that made her think of honey. The entire thing seemed like a collapse waiting to begin.

Regardless, the old woman moved through the clutter without hesitation. She was taller than Harriet and draped in black silk robes that clung to the bony frame underneath. Her cheeks were sunken but the skin was smooth and unblemished. Loose strands of dark hair that looked like it had been burned hung down and framed her face, blocking her eyes from view. Despite the lack of horrific witchy features, Harriet couldn't fight the shudder that passed through her. She retreated a step from the crone.

"I take it I've found Granny Wise," Harriet said.

"You've found nothing and no one, dearie," the woman said. "I showed myself to you. I didn't have to. Could have let you wander in the dark until dawn. Done it before, lots of times. Most make it home. Eventually. Sit, sit."

Granny Wise had moved to the other side of the table and lowered herself into a squat. Harriet looked for a stool or a pillow that looked sturdy enough to serve as a seat. Finding nothing, she crouched and rested her arms on her knees. Granny Wise had opened an oblong wooden box and was arranging colorful stones on a piece of cloth that was spread across the center of the table.

"I hear you have a way of... guiding fates."

The crone looked up, finally revealing her eyes. They were an unnatural blue, the eyes of a newborn child, startlingly large. Harriet rocked back on her heels and Granny Wise grinned.

"What do you seek, dear? Riches? You wish me to guide you to fortune? Do you want cohorts to whisper your name with fear and respect?"

Harriet shook her head, regaining her composure. "Any fortune I gain will be earned, as will my name. I need no shortcuts to either. I come to ask for the means."

"Tell me," Granny Wise said, drawing the two words out until they sounded like a song. She went back to sorting the stones.

"I want a ship," Harriet said. "I wish to be a captain, crewed by people *I* choose."

The gnarled hands hesitated. The woman looked up again. "Certainly there are easier ways to achieve these goals."

"Easy enough to get, sure," Harriet said. "And the crew wouldn't be hard to find. Keeping it. That's where the problem lies for anyone lacking a prod between their legs."

The hands went back to sorting the stones. Granny Wise held one that looked like clear glass with smears of black-and-purple liquid swirling inside. She closed her fingers around it and muttered quietly under her breath. She held the stone up and closed one eye, using the other to peer at Harriet through the stone.

"You wish for respect."

"I'm not asking to be charmed. I don't aim to be invincible or unbreakable. I'll escape any dangers with my wits and courage or I'll have a death I deserve. I'll earn fame and fortune, or fail, on my own merits. All I ask is that my crew and I are judged by those merits and not our gender."

Granny Wise said, "Treated as any man would be in the same situation."

"Until my reputation can speak for itself," Harriet said.

"Hm." Granny Wise licked her lips and nodded slowly. "Big work. Heavy impact. Could change your entire future. Requires changing the behavior of everyone you meet. Hundreds of hearts and minds."

Harriet nodded. "I understand the weight of what I'm asking."

"And you understand the cost will be high."

"Yes."

Granny Wise breathed in deeply and held the air in her chest, seeming to expand like a jellyfish. When she finally exhaled, the reek that rode on her breath made Harriet's eyes water.

"I can do this. I will clear the path to a ship. I will guide the feet of your crew to harbors where you can find them. Fame and fortune will be yours to seek. You will have to fight for it, and your enemies will still be many."

Harriet's hands tingled and she struggled to keep her breath steady. "Yes. That is what I want."

"Do not agree until you hear the cost."

Harriet had feared this moment. She reached for the pouch on her belt. Though her family had always had money, it had been years since she was allowed unfettered access to it. And even before the ties were cut, she had never carried this much gold on her person before.

"I've sold as much as I can. I've taken some as well. If there needs to be more, I can~"

"Hold your coin," Granny Wise said. "I have no need for gold. The island gives me more than I could ever use in a lifetime. I want something more precious than shine that can be given and taken on a whim."

Harriet furrowed her brow. "I have nothing else to give, Granny Wise."

The old woman laughed. It sounded like stones falling on wood. "I require your soul, girl."

"My..."

"Not now. You will live your life, natural and with no interference. I will not number your days. But when you die, your soul will come to me." She held up the black-and-purple stone.

"And I will have the life and experiences of a sea captain. I will have the chance to see the world through her eyes. I will ride the waves, fight battles, earn fortunes."

Harriet said, "Is that possible?"

Granny Wise laughed and waved her hand toward the walls. Harriet saw dozens of stones on shelves there.

"I have been a scholar. I have ventured deep into the subcontinent. I have experienced things that most mortal men would call impossible. I have been a father and a mother. And I have died, oh, thirty times by now. I stopped counting long ago. I have been evil. I have been beloved. Killed and comforted. But I have never lived a life at sea. Hm, yes. It intrigues me."

"And my life is my own until then?"

"The same as it would be without our bargain," Granny Wise said. "I am no devil and I will not require payment after a certain span of years. Your life and your death will be wholly your own."

Harriet didn't believe in the soul. She didn't believe in any afterlife. If the old woman thought there was something worth catching from her final breath, she didn't see the harm in it.

"Very well, Granny." Harriet held out her hand. "We have an accord."

Granny Wise suddenly sat up very straight, her chin held up so high that she had to look down her nose at Harriet. A cold wind swept into the structure, so strong that it made the walls shudder. The glass bottles clattered against each other, and the stones jittered on the table. Granny Wise threw herself across the table with both arms outstretched. Harriet tried to escape her reach, but the old woman was shockingly fast.

One hand went to the back of Harriet's head. The other clapped over her mouth. She felt something hard and smooth press against her lips. She fought against it, but Granny Wise was terribly strong and only pressed harder. Only when it touched her tongue did Harriet realize it was the black and purple stone. She gagged, but Granny Wise kept her hand in place.

Their faces were close enough that Harriet could see her reflection in those unnatural eyes. The light dimmed until Granny Wise was nothing but a silhouette. It only occurred to Harriet in that moment that she never saw the source of the light, nor had she understood how the glow had gone unseen until she was at the threshold of the hovel.

"Your soul upon your death," Granny Wise hissed. Now her

voice was an animal sound.

Harriet choked out an affirmative response.

"Swear to me, Harriet Landau."

She'd never told the crone her name, and yet was unsurprised that she would know it. There were tears in her eyes, both from terror and from choking on the stone.

I swear it, she thought.

The wind howled, or maybe it was Granny Wise, and the shriek reached a pitch that was agony to Harriet's ears. The crone said something - a mantra, a chant, a spell - but Harriet's mind was too muddled to make any sense of it, or even determine if it was English.

And then the stone was gone from her mouth. The lights completely extinguished as the weight of the crone lifted up off her body as if the woman had taken flight.

Harriet screamed and fell onto her back into the sand.

Her entire body jerked with her return to wakefulness, kicking up sand from her hands and feet. The world swam in front of her, flashes of light and color that swirled in the wrong directions. The horizon looked curled around the sea with the sky in the center. Her brain seemed to think she was in a freefall despite feeling the ground underneath her. She swayed and put a hand over her eyes until she felt some version of steadiness return to the world.

It was day. Mid-afternoon, from what she could deduce by squinting through her fingers. Her stomach was twisted. She tried to remember how much she'd drunk the night before. There weren't any bottles in the sand around her, which was good. Also no signs that she had been sick while she was passed out, which was always a good way to wake up.

She planted her feet flat on the ground and pushed, testing her legs. They seemed strong enough to hold her up, so she slowly got up and looked around.

The tavern where she'd been drinking the night before was about fifty yards down the beach. She must have gotten absolutely blotto and then stumbled out the door in search of Granny Wise. She thanked whatever gods looked out for seafaring fools that she'd only made it this far before she passed out and had that crazy dream. The wilds could be fatal even to sober wanderers once the sun went down.

Harriet tugged her sleeves down. That was when she noticed

the black ink on her skin. She pulled the sleeve away and held the arm up to frown at the design. A thin line encircled her entire left forearm just below the elbow. Thicker ribbons extended from the line, trailing up to over her elbow to wrap around her bicep like the tentacles of a kraken.

She brushed the design with her thumb. It didn't smear, and it wasn't sore. The skin around the markings wasn't sensitive or swollen to indicate it was a new tattoo.

"Bollocks," she muttered. She'd hoped to get a few actual voyages under her belt before she was inked up. She didn't want anyone to think she was claiming experience she didn't have. She wrinkled her lip at her drunk decision and pulled the sleeve down over her design. At least it could be easily hidden.

There was a ship in the harbor that would be heading out soon. She intended to be on it. Her dream had been absolute madness, but there had been a grain of truth in it. Whatever fame or fortune awaited her on the sea, she intended to earn it for herself.

And if, when her life was over, her soul ended up in the withered hands of a witch, well... she would just make sure the crone got one hell of a show.

CHAPTER ONE

Islas Baleares
Thirty-odd years later

CAPTAIN CLIO Landau squinted as she stepped out onto the deck of the *Banshee*, pausing to let her eyes adjust to the harsh Mediterranean sun before she continued onward. She was conflicted by her reaction to the silence and stillness of the ship. In a deep down part of her, she felt that being safe in a harbor was contradictory to a ship like this. Its sails needed to breathe with the wind, its hull needed to cut through strong waves. The wood needed to creak and groan with the power of fighting back against the sea. Sitting in port was the same as caging a wild animal and expecting the beast to be happy about it.

But on the other hand, she appreciated the peace that came with standing still. She liked stepping out onto the deck and knowing exactly what she would see: the hazy line where powder blue sky met cobalt sea to the south, the towering rocky cliffs capped with thick forest to the north. There was something to be said for a modicum of familiarity. It wasn't enough to make her set down roots anywhere; she would never be content to just sit in one place and let the world roll on around her. But every now and then she could understand the appeal.

The ship also felt abandoned, due to half the crew being on shore leave. She had considered joining them, but she'd been wary of liquor since she discovered the truth of who she'd once been. It had been thirty years since she went by the name Alice Malyns, since she'd prowled the seas hunting pirates and sentencing them to the gallows. As far as she was concerned, that person was dead and buried. But now that the memories had been unlocked, however distant they might feel, she couldn't risk lowering her walls and tempting fate.

Clio went to the railing and looked out at the island. *Las Islas Baleares* had been a favorite downtime destination for Harriet. She suggested spending time there at least twice per year, when they were in the area and could afford a few days of leisure. Clio always eagerly agreed. They would find a nice hut isolated from the rest of the crew and spend a few days enjoying the benefits of solid ground and a soft bed. The island was as close to home as anything to Harriet. It was her source, the sacred place where she had set off on her life of piracy.

For a few years after Harriet passed, the idea of coming back was far too painful to entertain. Too many memories lingering on those beaches and hidden in those thick forests. Even after that pain faded, returning without Harriet felt wrong, too much like a betrayal to visit without the woman who had introduced it to her.

But then Clio received a message, passed from one hand to another, from boat to island to ship, until it reached its final destination in her hands. A summons, from a man she remembered very well.

Her initial instinct had been to ignore it. But it felt safer to come back now. The crew had made their own memories on this rocky little archipelago, and she was starting to feel bad for denying them a return. So, because they happened to be in the area and had no pressing business elsewhere, she gave the order to bring them back. It felt good to be here again, it felt like turning back a few pages to a different time in her life.

But despite feeling ready, despite the fact she believed she could handle whatever emotions were stirred by being back here, she still couldn't bring herself to leave the ship.

She had seen the launch on its way back from port, but she'd assumed it was just crewmembers returning for a clean shirt, extra coin, or a quick rest in a familiar bed. As it grew closer, however, she noted the tall man seated at the stern. She recognized him immediately and laughed despite herself. She slapped the wood of the railing, put her thumb and forefinger between her lips, and let out a long, shrill whistle. The man twisted at the waist, nearly upturning the boat, then stood up and held his arms out wide in greeting.

"Cl-i-i-i-oh-oh-oh!"

Santiago Zeno's bellow echoed off the tall cliffs that surrounded the harbor. He clapped his beefy hands together in delight. His exuberance caused the launch to rock again and the woman rowing - Clio could see now that it was her first mate, Fausta Gittens - scolded him. Whatever she'd said was hard enough and carried enough truth that he dropped back down onto the bench and drew his arms in close.

Clio moved away from the railing and went back to her quarters. She retrieved a bottle of El Lloar, a local red wine, and set it on her table with two glasses. After a moment she added a third, in case Fausta wished to stay for the conversation. She had just enough time to raid her stash of food for a block of cheese and crackers to accompany their drinks before she heard the launch arrive. There was a shattering of voices on the deck as crewmembers saw their visitor and swarmed him with greetings.

Once he had cleared the scrum of well-wishing old friends, Santiago stepped through her office door. He was even taller than she remembered, able to stand up straight in the cabin but with very little clearance between his salt-and-pepper hair and the timber of the ceiling. His shoulders were broad from years of rowing back and forth to ships.

Clio grinned when she saw him, and he unleashed another bellowing laugh. He held his arms out to her bent his knees to wrap his arms around her. She was crushed in the hug, her face pressed to his shirt. He smelled of salt and sea air, and a little of maleness that put her off, but she maintained her smile until he let her go.

She slapped his arms as hard as she could, stinging her palms and affecting him not at all. "Santy! It's been too long."

"Far too long," he said, scrutinizing the short blonde spikes of her hair. "You've gotten old, Clio. Congratulations. It suits you."

"And to you," Clio said. "Come, sit, we must catch up."

"Yes! We must!" He turned to confirm Fausta was still behind him. She was leaning against the doorframe, apparently content to silently observe. "I was very nervous to ask Miz Gittens here if you were still in command of the *Banshee*. I'd seen it in the harbor and had horrible thoughts about what might have transpired since your last visit. Imagine my immense relief when she told me you were still the ruler of this roost. Followed by immense sadness to know you chose to spend so long away from our shores."

Clio nodded. "It was difficult. Harriet... adored it here."

Santiago's mood immediately softened. He folded his hands in front of him and bowed his head. "Aye, yes. She is sorely missed. And she is also the reason I was so desperate to see you again."

"So you felt the need to summon me?"

"Ah no. For that, I had a very specific reason to bring you back here." He fished around in his pocket until he found a small leather bag. He loosened the strap that held it shut, explaining as he extracted the item. "This island has its myths and legends. Ghosts and faery stories. One of the most often-told was the tale of Granny Wise."

Clio nodded. "I know that one. Harriet told me about it. She had a dream of Granny Wise the night before she became a pirate." She smiled sadly. "She always said she believed it was the spirit of the sea calling out to her."

Santiago dug inside the pouch with his fingers. "Mm, mm, maybe so, maybe. But two months ago, thereabouts, someone found a hovel in the forest. A shack built around the mouth of a cave, more shelter than an actual home." The pouch held several stones, apparently, and he continued searching for one in particular. "They went inside and found the body of an old woman. She hadn't been dead long when they found her, but there was no hope of reviving."

"That's terrible," Clio said solemnly. "Dying alone like that."

"Mm, mm," Santiago said again. "Well, they found all kinds of gewgaws around. Gathered 'em up, brought it all to town. Started trading it all for drinking money. I bought up what I could. Figured I could maybe make a lot more selling to passing ships.

"I won't pretend like I know what any of it was or does. But there these were stones. And Granny Wise was said to use stones as a medium for her magic. Don't know anything about that, either, but it's what folks said. So there were stones, and an old woman dead in the forest. It was enough for most people around here to say that the witch woman of the forest had met her end."

"That makes sense."

He held out one of the stones and Clio took it. She'd never seen anything like it. The swirling shades of red and purple gave it an odd depth, as if it was made of glass, but when she turned it in her fingers, she could see that it was a trick of the eye. There was a design of a sun emitting wavy lines like a crown of wild snakes.

"Aha!" Santiago held up the stone he'd been seeking. "This is why I've been eager to see you again. Well, one of the reasons. Always a pleasure to see you, Captain Clio. But..." He held out the stone and Clio traded the first for it. At first she was distracted by the colors again - black and purple on this one - but then she noticed the design.

"This is Harriet's tattoo."

Santiago nodded, suddenly somber. "Aye. Unmistakable, that, even though it's been ages since I seen her. But I recognized it right off. I don't know if she based her ink off that, or if Granny Wise copped it from Harriet. I suppose one way is just as likely as the other, considering how much time Harriet spent here."

Clio ran her thumb over the design. She'd seen the tattoo thousands of times, had kissed it and pressed her face against it. She'd never asked Harriet what it meant or where it came from. She assumed Harriet would have told her if there was any special meaning. It was the only tattoo she had, so Clio had just accepted it was a memorial to someone or other, and left it at that. But now, seeing it on this stone, she hated herself for not asking more questions.

"How much?"

Santiago shook his head. "No, no. As I said, I've been holding that for you. It is meant to be with you. I would feel wrong selling it."

Clio folded her fingers around the stone. It felt cold against her palm. "Thank you, Santiago."

He inclined his head to her. He looked past her at the wine and cheese, then arched an eyebrow. "Have I been keeping you from fancy guests?"

"That was for you."

"No, no, no," he said. "For the likes of me? An oaf such as myself only merits coconut juice and stale chunks of bread, surely!"

Clio laughed and retrieved the bottle. "If you won't accept payment, then accept a gift in return." She held the bottle out to him. "With my blessing."

Santiago began to demur, then tilted his head. He took the bottle and then glanced sideways at Fausta.

"Would it be incredibly rude if I were to... partake of this elsewhere?"

"Elsewhere?" Clio looked at Fausta, then at Santiago. She raised her eyebrows. "Oh! With... together? Of course. With my blessing."

He grinned. "Thank you, Captain Clio." He leaned in and kissed her cheek. His stubble scratched her skin as he pulled back. "It is wonderful to see you again. And you truly do wear the years well. May you continue to improve with age."

"I'm starting to understand how you got aboard this ship, sweet talker. Go on."

He left the cabin, glancing back to Fausta. She motioned for him to keep going, then stepped closer to Clio. She crossed her arms over her chest, obviously deciding she would take the interrogation now rather than later.

"Really, Fausta?" Clio asked under her breath. "With a man?"

"On occasion."

Clio glanced toward the empty corridor. "That occasion...?"

Fausta grinned. "There have been worse occasions. He's handsome. Strong. Tall. Spanish." She shrugged. "Lobster is far from my favorite meal, but sometimes it's nice to remind myself why it's still on the menu."

Clio snickered. "Go. Enjoy my wine."

Fausta saluted and hurried to catch up with Santiago. Clio shut the cabin door behind her and went to the window behind her desk. She held up the stone, Harriet's stone, so that it caught the sunlight coming through the weathered glass. It glistened in a way she'd never seen a mundane stone shine. At one angle, it seemed like any other rock. But turning it ever so slightly... a gleam.

"Very curious," she said under her breath.

If Granny Wise had still been among the living, and in that state been obliged to explain, she would have revealed the ritual of the stones was really quite simple. A soul was a wild, wandering thing and it was eager to escape confinement. The prison of a body, or of a stone. Releasing one required holding the stone close and focusing on the soul it contained. Once there was a solid connection, the stone required its recipient to have a clear mind. This was most easily accomplished with liquor, hallucinogens, or, her favorite method, a superb orgasm. If she chose to access the memories in a stone, she would get drunk off wine or berries, then pleasure herself with one hand while she clutched the stone in the other and focused on its passenger.

So it was aboard the *Banshee* on that sunny day off the coastline of a Spanish island. Clio lay in her bed and ran her fingers over the mysterious design she'd spent thirty years admiring on her wife's arm. Harriet had always covered it with her sleeves, so it was likely only a handful of crew had ever seen it. Knowledge of the ink was restricted to only a handful of Harriet's most precious people, and Clio appreciated the reminder that she had been among that number. She had been Harriet's favorite person in the world, her One.

Tears filled Clio's eyes. She brought the stone to her forehead. She cried and, quietly, whispered, "Harriet..." The name seemed to have an unusual snap to it, seemed to carry more weight than usual, so she said it again. "Harriet." Suddenly it was more than just a name, more than a simple word. It was a mantra, a prayer. Something sacred. "Harriet. Harriet..."

Simultaneously, two decks below, Fausta Gittens was in the midst of using a very willing Santiago Zeno to scratch a few itches that she hadn't satisfied for many years. The poor man had no idea what he was subjecting himself to when he began flirting with the pretty Persian pirate, and he seemed thrilled to find himself far, far out of his league. He held onto her hips and tried to keep pace, but she was no match for him.

His eyes rolled back in his head.

Two decks above, Clio squeezed the stone and whispered, "Harriet Landau."

Santiago saw stars when he orgasmed, then he saw blackness.

And then he saw nothing.

CHAPTER TWO

FAUSTA TRIED not to be offended when Santiago suddenly threw her to the side. He coughed as he rolled away from her. He had one hand on his throat while the other gripped the sheet so hard it untucked it at the sides. Fausta could see his entire body shake with the force of his coughing. It sounded like he was choking on a stone larger than the one he'd given to Clio.

"Are you all right?" she asked.

"I'm ch~" Another violent cough, this one sending him to his feet. "I can't... I..." He made a roaring growl sound, then rubbed at his throat with the web between his thumb and forefinger. "Something is wrong," he croaked. "I-I ca-can't... I..." Another violent cough.

Fausta had climbed off the bed and wriggled into his shirt. She had stepped into her own trousers and sinched them tight as she approached him.

"Do you need me to get the doctor? I think Delfina is still aboard."

"Delfina... De~" Another choking sound. "Delfina is here?"

Fausta tried to remember if she'd stayed aboard or gone ashore. "I can go look. I'm pretty sure she opted to stay. Do you know what's wrong?"

"Wrong? I was hung! Christ, my throat! Why does my voice sound like this!" He cleared his throat violently, baring his teeth. "Was my neck broken?"

"Not that I noticed," Fausta said.

"My voice. My god, what's..."

Fausta wrapped a sheet around his waist and tucked it in, hopefully with a knot secure enough to keep it in place for the journey to the infirmary.

"Come on. Let's go find out what the fuck just happened to you."

She managed to get Santiago through the door and up the stairs to the deck. When they hit sunshine he hissed and covered his eyes. He turned his head away and saw her in full light for the first time.

"Fausta...?"

"Well done, lad. You've done better than most of the men who have been in your position. Even they would have at least tried to let me finish as well, though."

"Wait. What are~" His legs buckled and he hit the deck.

Fausta swore under her breath. "Captain! Someone get the captain and Doc Pendergast!"

"The captain?" Santiago rasped. "Good god, what is ha-happ~" He coughed again. "Everything feels wrong, Fausta. I c-can't... see right, everything feels..."

Clio appeared and crossed the deck. "Fausta? What happened? What did he do?"

Santiago's head snapped up at the sound of her voice. "Clio," he gasped. His eyes were open, but the muscles around them were tight. It was clear he was trying and for some reason failing to see. "Clio, is that you?"

"He didn't do anything," Fausta said. "Not even what I dragged him down there to do, honestly. But when he was finished he started having some kind of fit. Coughing and clutching at his throat."

"Who are you talking about?" Santiago asked.

Clio both looked at him. She bent forward to line up their eyes. She could almost see the fog lifting. His eyes relaxed, and a smile curled the corners of his lips. When he spoke again, his voice was soft and unstrained.

"Clio, what's happening to me?"

"I'd like to know the same thing, Santy."

He furrowed his brow. "Santy? You mean Santiago Zeno...?"

"Yes..." Clio said.

Santiago looked at Fausta. "Is he..." Behind her, he spotted the cliffs. "Islas Baleares... why are we here? Does this have something to do with Granny Wise?"

Delfina arrived at that moment. She apprised the situation, a half-naked man wrapped in a sheet kneeling on the deck, and assumed she knew what had happened. "How badly did you hurt him, Fausta?"

"I didn't do shit. He didn't do shit. He got his rocks off, but barely even got started on the things I wanted him to do."

"He may be suffering memory loss," Clio said. "Doesn't seem to know his own name."

"I know my name," Santiago said, his confusion fading into anger. "Who is this man you're talking about?"

Delfina had frozen, staring down at Santiago's arms, folded in his lap. "Clio. His arm. Look at his arm."

Clio and Fausta both looked. The black line of a tattoo wrapped around the forearm, just below his elbow. Waving flags hung from the line.

"He didn't have that before," Fausta said.

Clio looked at Santiago again. "You said you knew your name." Her voice wavered. "Say and prove it."

Santiago looked at them, confusion reigning again.

"My name is Harriet Landau," he snapped. "And as your captain, I *demand* to know what you are all talking about!"

Delfina and Fausta looked at Clio, whose face had drained of color. Santiago looked at her as well.

"Clio. What is..."

"Damn it, just look at yourself," Fausta snapped.

Santiago looked at her, then looked down at himself. He held his hands out and stared at them, curled the fingers, twisted the wrists to look at the palms. He extended his arms and his gaze extended to his bare chest, which rose and fell with increasing speed. He slapped a hand against his shoulder and then looked at Delfina with panic in his eyes. He started to speak, but then his body went slack and he fell forward.

Clio caught his shoulder and Delfina pressed her hands against his chest to prevent him from hitting the deck.

"He's passed out."

"Given the circumstances, I can't say I blame him," Fausta said.

They summoned a few deckhands to help carry him to the infirmary. When he'd been taken away, Fausta snapped her fingers in front of Clio's unfocused eyes to bring her back out of her head.

"I've got no idea what happened," Fausta said, answering the only question Clio could've asked at that point. "I assume it's got something to do with that rock and the story he was spinning when he got here. Did you do anything with it?"

Clio's eyes swept from side to side as if she was trying to remember some long-ago event. "I held it," she said, her voice choked. "I just... I was holding it."

"Well, apparently there was some kind of real magic at work with Granny Wise. I'll head back to the island and see what I can dig up."

"Thank you." She looked up as if suddenly realizing her first mate was there. "You... what were you, um..." She gestured. "In case Delfina asks."

Fausta said, "We were... half finished, if you catch my meaning."

"So he had~"

"He was in the midst when he suddenly started going savage." She looked in the direction Delfina and Santiago had vanished. "You don't think it's... There's no chance it's actually~"

"I haven't got a clue." Clio didn't want to hear the end of that question. Even speaking it aloud would be too close to letting herself hope. "Right now I don't know if I want it to be true or if I'm praying it's a cruel hoax. I've known Santy a long time, and I don't think he would do something like this. And he looked genuinely confused and terrified."

Fausta nodded. "Whatever the truth is, we'll find answers one way or another."

"And sooner rather than later," Clio said. "Find Ranzi and get her to help. And... Baillie. She could be useful in finding information."

"Aye, Captain."

Fausta headed for the launch. When she looked back, Clio still hadn't moved, but she was staring in the direction of the infirmary like it was the most treacherous place she could ever travel.

Clio stopped in the doorway of the infirmary and looked in. Only two lanterns had been lit on either side of the bed, so most of the room was cast in deep shadows. The man on the bed was illuminated with an almost other-worldly glow. He had been dressed in a shirt and a pair of slacks. He was awake but looked stunned. His eyes were wide and constantly scanning the room, lips pressed together so hard that they were trembling. Delfina was checking his pulse, a look of consternation on her face.

Clio gave up on the idea of preparing herself for what she had to do and stepped into the room. Delfina and Santiago both looked at her. His eyes were wide, desperate. She'd never seen him look at her that way. She'd seen that look in other eyes, but she refused to assign them to a memory. She tore her gaze away from his and focused on Delfina instead.

"He seems to be in good health," she said. "He's in a panic, clearly, but I can't find anything physically wrong with him. No bump on the head, no fresh wounds..."

"Could you please stop referring to me as 'him'?" Santiago said.

Clio said, "We're not going to call you Harriet."

"But I'm... that's..." He closed his eyes and clenched his jaw. It was another familiar gesture. Seeing it stabbed ice into Clio's heart. She took a step back from the bed, her hands in fists at her sides so she wouldn't be tempted to reach out.

"What's the last thing you remember?" Delfina asked softly.

Santiago narrowed his eyes. "I was captured with Ranzi and Aravanis. We were set to be hanged. Clio..." She looked over at her. "She came back with Fausta to break us out. Succeeded, too. Did a hell of a job and made me proud. But we were cornered. Cut off from the ship. The constables would've grabbed all of us. So I made a decision. I knew they'd chase me, so I shot one of them and ran. I didn't regret it for a second, even as they looped the rope around my neck. It gave my..." He looked at Clio, then away. "It gave my crew the opportunity to escape."

Clio's throat threatened to close up. She was finding it hard to draw breath. She looked at the wall above Santiago's bed. No one, bar a handful of crewmembers of this boat, knew the story of how Harriet died, or why. Cariad Baillie knew, but Clio didn't think she'd written it down yet. Even if she had, the book she was writing had never left the *Banshee*.

"Are you okay, Clio?" Delfina asked.

"Impossible question," Clio whispered. She forced herself to meet Santiago's eyes. "You asked if we were here because of Granny Wise. Why did you make that leap?"

Santiago pushed himself up higher in the bed. "I always

thought it was a dream, but I guess I really did find her. I told her my greatest desire was this... a ship, respect, a crew of women. She told me I'd have it in exchange for my soul when I died. I never believed in any kind of afterlife, so it seemed like a solid deal. But if I was really hanged... and if..." She looked at Clio. "How did you know about the deal? A-and how did you get her to give you the stone? And why, in god's name, did you put me in Santy's body? Of all people..."

"Harriet," Clio said. "We didn't know. We just happened to come here. Santiago had the stone because he found it in Granny Wise's things after she... a-after she died. He recognized your tattoo design on the stone, so he gave it to me. We had no idea about any of this. We're as shocked as you are."

Delfina said, "Probably a touch more shocking to the woman who just came back from the dead in a man's body."

Clio absently nodded her agreement.

"Is..." Delfina furrowed her brow and searched for the right way to phrase her next question. "Is Santiago still there? Inside, or...?"

"I don't know. I don't know what it would feel like if he..." His voice trailed off. "Yes. Actually, I can tell. He's here. I can hear him. It's like it's... like I'm in a house, and he's talking in another room, and he can only come to where I am if I go to another room. Oh, that is... very strange... The faster we can figure out how to get me into the right body, the better."

Clio tensed. "What?"

Santiago looked at her. "My body. I-I assume... oh. Were you not able to retrieve it? That makes sense. That island was a fortress."

"No, Harriet, we..."

Her mouth was dry. She realized she had just referred to this man by her wife's name. It had felt right. She realized she'd been seeing him as Harriet for a while by that point. It was her mannerisms, the way she spoke, the way she looked at Clio. There was nothing in the person on the bed who made her think of Santiago.

Delfina touched Harriet's hand. "I'm sorry, dear. We were able to retrieve your body. We gave you a proper funeral. A burial at sea. Eight years ago."

Harriet shuddered and put her hands over her face. "No."

"I'm so sorry." Delfina stepped away from the bed. "I'll give you two some time."

Clio watched her leave. Then, uncertain of what else to do, she gingerly sat down on the side of the bed. Harriet seemed to be crying softly behind her hands. Clio scanned the darkness around them, hoping for some inspiration of what to say. She started to speak once, then twice, then pressed her lips together.

"Eight years," Harriet said from behind her hands.

Clio's eyes burned with tears. "I've missed you. So much."

Harriet sniffled and held out a hand.

Clio stared at it. The odd, thick fingers. The unfamiliar shape. But she held it out the same way Harriet used to: at a slight angle, the index and middle fingers extended with the ring and pinky slightly curled back toward the palm. After a moment she lifted her own hand, slipped it into Harriet's, and heaved a sob when those strange fingers curled tight.

CHAPTER THREE

CARIAD BAILLIE pulled the chair out from beneath the desk and hefted it, aiming the four legs at the villain that had cornered her. She knew it was a paltry defense, but it was all she had. "Stay back, ye filthy pirate." Her Scottish brogue was thick and almost indecipherable. "I'm warning ye. One more step and I'll scream."

"No one's coming to save you," the dreaded pirate said, taking one more step closer to Cariad. "My crew's taken care of everyone else. And now you're all... mine, to do... with as I..." Estacia Navarro sighed and her shoulders slumped. "Are you sure about this?"

Cariad straightened and rested her hands on the back of the chair. "Is it too far?" Her accent had softened back to its normal, softened edges.

"Well, it's..." Estacia shrugged and held her hands out. "It's... forceful."

"Right. At first. You rip off my clothes and throw me on the bed. And you pin me down. And, and... but *then* I succumb to the rogue's kisses, and her gentle hands." Just thinking about it was enough to make her breathe harder. She felt a burning in her cheeks. "And I let the pirate have her way with me."

"I'm a cook."

"On a pirate ship."

"And we don't do this sort of shit. Ever."

"No, of course not." Cariad tucked her red hair behind her ears. "I'm sorry. I thought maybe it would be fun. A little roughness, a little..." She balled her hands into fists and mimicked a push-pull. "But without the fear of things getting out of hand because of the trust. I trust you. Mostly because we're standing here having this conversation. Again."

Estacia smiled bashfully. "I want to give you what you want. But it's very hard being the aggressor in a situation like this."

"Of course." Cariad picked up the chair and put it back under the desk. She went to Estacia and cupped her face. "Thank you for even trying. I know it makes you uncomfortable. I appreciate you trying. It means a lot to me." She gave Estacia a tender kiss. "Come on. Let's go back to the bar. I'll buy you a drink, sailor."

She started to walk away, but Estacia grabbed Cariad's hand and pulled her back. "Where d'ye think yer going, schoolmarm?"

"Wha... I..."

"I didn't excuse you yet."

Estacia grabbed a handful of Cariad's shirt and pulled her forward in a brutal kiss. Cariad yelped, slapped her hands against Estacia's chest, and wriggled in an attempt to get free. She ignored the brief moments when she actually did get free, moving her arm back until Estacia could grip it again. Estacia guided her toward the bed and tossed her onto the mattress.

"You'll pay for this, ye brute!" Cariad hissed, her brogue back in place.

"I think I'll be takin' my reward now, lassy." Estacia grabbed the two sides of Cariad's shirt in her fists. She started to pull, then hesitated and looked up into Cariad's eyes. She whispered, "You said to tear. Tear your clothes. Did you mean *actually* tear~"

"Yes," Cariad whispered. "I have another pair."

Estacia nodded and ripped the shirt open. Cariad was topless underneath, and Estacia pressed her face between her lover's breasts. She licked a familiar trail, following a ladder of freckles to one pink nipple. She closed her lips around it, sucking until it was hard enough to capture with her teeth.

Cariad put her arms over her head. "You beast," she said, wrapping her legs around Estacia's waist. "You monster!"

"I'll show you a monster." She sat up and Cariad's legs fell away, framing Estacia as she grabbed the belt buckle and tugged it free.

She got Cariad's pants down and tossed them aside. She sank to her knees and pushed Cariad's legs apart. She wet her lips and then bent forward to drag her tongue from Cariad's knee up the inside of her thigh. Cariad gasped and grabbed a handful of Estacia's thick hair. She threw her head back and rested her feet on Estacia's shoulders.

"You... b-brute," she gasped. And then, eyes rolling back in her head, she lost the ability to keep up the game. She bit her bottom lip and squeezed her eyes shut. Estacia had one hand underneath Cariad, cupping her buttocks, while the other worked its way back to Cariad's breast, letting her thumb and forefinger take over while her lips and tongue were otherwise occupied.

She was right on the verge of orgasm when the door of their room swung open and Fausta stepped in. Cariad yelped and tugged the ripped halves of her shirt over her chest with one hand. Estacia remained where she was. She cupped her hand over Cariad's mound to hide it from view, but the pressure risked doing more harm than good. Cariad tensed and bit her bottom lip.

Fausta raised an eyebrow and half-turned, raising her hand in a half-hearted attempt to hide her eyes. "Sorry to intrude, but we need the writer."

"I-I-I..."

Estacia said, "Five minutes?" Her lips and chin were shining and, despite the circumstances, the sight caused a shiver to pass under Estacia's palm.

Fausta looked like she wanted to protest, but then she nodded. "Hell, why not. If it makes you feel better, I had a good time cut short, too."

She stepped back out into the corridor and pulled the door shut behind her.

Estacia faced forward again and moved her hand. She licked her lips and leaned in.

"Wait," Cariad gasped. Her heart was pounding from the fear and excitement of almost being caught. "Hold on." She swept her hair back. The sweat on her face felt cold. "C-can we just... go right back to things...?"

"I don't know. You tell me."

A few seconds later, Cariad was positive they could absolutely get right back to things.

Fausta was leaning against the wall across from the door, arms folded over her chest, turned to face toward the harbor. Cariad blushed as she came out, still tucking her spare, unripped shirt into her trousers. Her face was flush and sweaty from sex, but Estacia had taken the time to lovingly wash her thighs before putting her pants back on.

"You could have waited farther away," Cariad said.

"I wouldn't have been able to hear from further away."

Cariad's cheeks burned. "You listened?"

Fausta grinned. "It's a small ship, Baillie, and you two have been excitable little rabbits. We've *all* heard you."

"Devil mend you," Cariad muttered. Then she decided she wasn't going to dwell on it. "What was so all-fired important, then?"

"Come on. We're on a hunt." She started walking and Cariad followed. "We need to find out everything we can about a witch who used to ply her trade on this island. I figured it would help to have a bookish type for the search." She glanced back the way they'd come. "Hopefully Estacia wasn't too upset about being left behind like that."

"I owe her a debt," Cariad said.

"From what I've heard on the ship, I'm sure she'll be repaid in full."

Cariad's blush deepened. "Why are we looking for a witch? I thought coming here was supposed to be for rest and recuperation."

"There's been a development on the ship. It's..." She blew out air through pursed lips. "I'll be honest, Baillie, I can't make heads or tails of it. I need some time before I try explaining it to you. For now, you just need to know we're looking for anyone who knows anything about Granny Wise or stones with strange markings on them."

"If you say so," Cariad said.

They had descended the stairs while they talked. When they reached the street, Fausta held her hands out to indicate the town.

"Okay. So where do you suggest we begin?"

"For myths and local legends?" Cariad screwed her lips to one side. "I assume this island doesn't have much in the way of libraries or museums. That means the best place to start would be taverns." She pointed toward the harbor and started walking.

"Really? We're going to rely on a bunch of drunkards to have answers for us?"

Cariad shrugged. "*In vino historia.*" When Fausta looked sideways at her, she said, "Yes. Bars, pubs, taverns. That's where this type of story tends to be spread in places like that. People get drunk and they're more likely to talk about the deep, shameful secrets of their home to strangers who come nosing around asking questions."

Fausta said, "I suppose I've found that to be true. It's just under the circumstances it would be best if our source of information was a bit more... reliable."

"The development you mentioned," Cariad said. "Is everyone in the crew okay? Is someone sick, or was there~"

"No, the crew is fine," Fausta said. "It's not a sickness. Or an injury. Nothing like that. I've never even heard of anything like it."

"Okay, that's fair. But I'm going to need some idea of what we're looking for if I'm going to help you dig up information. You mentioned the witch. Granny Wise, I think? I've heard her mentioned a few times. She's a real person?"

"Was," Fausta said. "Apparently she died. Santiago... that's Santiago Zeno, a friend of the captain... said an old woman's body was found in the forest surrounded by all kinds of strange dross. It's enough to make folks around here believe it was her. But for my part, I hope she's still kicking. We could definitely use her help." They had arrived at the first tavern, which was bustling despite being mid-afternoon. Fausta spotted a bottle on a nearby table and picked it up, checked the contents, then wiped the mouth. "Just ask about Granny Wise. See what people know about her, if anyone believes the body wasn't hers, that sort of thing. Oh. And anything about Santiago. If he has a base of operations or a business or anything we can search. He said he bought up a bunch of her things. Might be something useful among the haul."

"I can do that." She furrowed her brow, tilting her head to one side. "Santiago is a friend of the captain, isn't he? And he's..." She looked toward the harbor. She could see the *Banshee* calmly waiting in the distance. "Okay. If you can't explain the situation, you can at least tell me how bad the situation is on the ship."

"You'd think that," Fausta said. "It remains to be seen. Go on. Quick as you can."

"You are very light on the helpfulness, Fausta," Cariad muttered."

Fausta shrugged. "We're all adrift on this one, writer-girl." She went to a table at the back, taking a swig from her captured bottle as she went.

Cariad watched her go, then looked around hoping for inspiration of where to begin. Finally, with no other ideas, she walked up to the bar and fished for coins in her pockets. She realized she was wearing Estacia's trousers and made a silent promise to pay back whatever she spent. She held up the coins so the bartender could see them, then slapped them down as she'd often seen Ranzi do when buying a round.

"I'm buying drinks for anyone who has a true story about Granny Wise."

The men on either side of her murmured and grunted amongst themselves. Finally one lifted his hand, turning to face her more fully.

"I got a story for you..."

Cariad motioned the bartender closer. "Let's hear it, then."

Ines Ranzi moved carefully down what she was generously calling a trail. She paused every few steps to look back the way she'd come. She wasn't terribly worried about getting lost out here. She was moving inland, so all she had to do was turn around and start walking the other way. If she hit the beach, she could navigate by the sun to get back to the harbor. Keeping track still made her feel a little better about how close the trees were, and how completely they were blocking out the sun.

This was supposed to be a relaxing stopover. No jobs, no scandals, just old friends in a familiar setting. Someplace they could unwind and spend some of the money they'd accrued the past few months. But now Fausta had told her to investigate some hidden burrow of a witch who probably didn't even exist. The woman they'd found had probably just been one of the many unfortunates who washed up on the shore of Baleares every day. She didn't have money for passage home, didn't have skills to make herself useful in town, so she made whatever shelter she could and scavenged for what she needed. She might have been the source of the Granny Wise legends, the reality behind all the whispers and sighting, but Ranzi doubted there was any truth to anything the people of this island claimed. Just a tragic story of an old crone whose candle finally went out.

She'd asked a few people in town where the woman's body had been found. They had been less than helpful. "Out there," one had said, nodding at the forest. Another had shrugged. "It's not like there's landmarks, lass. Trees and more trees, maybe a rock that looks like the rock right next to it." She'd asked them how far into the woods it was. "A mile, maybe more," one man said. Another had spoken over him and said it was just past the tree line.

So here she was. Instead of resting on the beach with a glass of alcohol and melting ice, wandering into the forest because Fausta said "something" had happened on the ship and the captain needed them to gather information. She would be absolutely livid if this was some sort of prank. Fausta wasn't the first person she would suspect of tricking her. But it also wasn't outside the realm of possibility. And if she didn't find something soon she would~

Her boot snapped something on the trail. She glanced down, expecting to see just another twig, but instead she saw two pieces of a jagged purple stone.

"Hello there," she said under her breath.

She crouched down and picked up one of the pieces. As she twisted it between her fingers, she saw something from the corner of her eye. When she turned her head, a section of the forest had opened up into an open space. It didn't seem likely she had missed it. For the past five minutes, her field of vision had been full of an unbroken veil of tree bark and leaves. But now there was a gap in the flora, and she could make out the shape of furniture in the darkness.

"Now we're getting somewhere."

Ranzi pocketed the shard and stood up, moving between the trees until she reached the... it was incorrect to call it a clearing. It was almost as if the trees had been bent back out of the way like they were just tall blades of grass. The gap was wide enough that Ranzi could stand up inside it. The base of the trees, which should have been a twisted mass of roots, was unnaturally flattened. Ranzi saw a table with cushions around it where she could sit if she had been so inclined. She saw jars, moldy and shrouded with cobwebs, the labels stuck to each one faded into uselessness.

It occurred to her only after she'd taken her quick inventory that she was, for all intents and purposes, inside a ball of trees. The path had been incredibly dark even before she found this hidden cove. It only seemed to have one entrance, and she was blocking it with her body. All those facts meant that there should have been no sunlight whatsoever spilling into this place.

"And yet, I can see it well," she muttered. "Strange..."

She decided she wouldn't suss out an answer about how the light was working in this place, so she continued her search. She found a leather-bound book on the table and thumbed through it. The pages were filled with the worst handwriting she'd ever seen.

The few phrases she was able to decipher seemed to be some kind of code, because the words made no sense in connection with the ones around it. She closed the book and tucked it into her belt. Someone else could go blind trying to make sense of it.

Ranzi gave one more look around the space. Something about it felt off. Unnatural, sure, but also extremely unwelcoming. She felt as if she had just walked into the parlor of some high-society toff and every eye in the room had turned toward her at the same time. It was like the room was screaming at her to *leave*. She was no welcome. She did not belong.

"All right," she said quietly, backing out of the eerie place. "You don't have to tell me twice."

Once she was back in the forest proper, making her way back toward the town, she looked over her shoulder to make sure nothing had emerged from the shadowy pit to pursue her.

She was not surprised to find the 'clearing' had completely vanished.

CHAPTER FOUR

THERE WAS no reason for Harriet to remain in the infirmary, since there was technically nothing wrong with her. The clothes Delfina had given her would do for now. Clio looked around for any spare boots or shoes, but she didn't find anything suitable. She doubted they had any footwear onboard that would fit her male feet anyway. She would have to wait until Fausta came back and retrieved Santiago's discarded clothes from her cabin before being fully dressed again.

They confirmed she could walk without leaning too heavily on Clio, then made their way up to the deck. Harriet hissed and covered her eyes when the sun hit her face.

"Damn. That happened last time I came above, too. I wonder if this man's eyes are over sensitive. Like sand in my eyes."

"Could be." Clio kept a hand on Harriet's arm, guiding her toward her cabin. "We should keep you out of sight until we know exactly what we're going to tell people."

Harriet nodded. "Seems smart. And I can stay here, at least for a while. Nobody on the island will miss Santiago. Not for a few days, at least."

Clio looked at her, surprised. "You... know that?"

"We're..." She narrowed her eyes and then grimaced. "Talking isn't the right word. But we're, we are in... contact. He knows what happened."

"How is he taking it?"

Harriet chuckled softly. "Poorly. But he also... understands. He knows that there's nowhere else for me to go. So for now I think he's content to let me, ah, borrow him."

"Let him know I appreciate that very much. Hopefully we can find a long-term solution that won't require him to sacrifice his body indefinitely."

"He's grateful."

When they reached her cabin, Clio got Harriet settled on the divan before she went back and closed the door.

"Fausta and Ranzi are on the island looking for any information they can find on Granny Wise. If there's a way to transfer you to another body, or-or some other solution."

Harriet smiled. "Nice to know some things have stayed the same, even though it's been so long since I was... here." She wet her lips. "And they accepted you as captain, I assume."

Clio nodded. "Oh yes. I tried to offer the position to Fausta, but she assured me she was happy enough serving me as she was you. She's a good quartermaster. And the best first mate I could ask for."

"Good. I'm glad." She stared down at her hands, flexing the fingers. "I assume there have been *some* crew changes. Who else is still around?"

"Well, you saw Delfina."

Harriet gave a small, nostalgic smile. "Aye. Growing more beautiful with every year, that one is. Hardly seems fair to the rest of us."

"Too true, too true. Estacia is still in charge of the mess."

"Ahh," she laughed. "It will be a joy to see her again."

"She's on the island now. Spending some quality time with her partner."

Harriet raised an eyebrow. "True?"

"Mm. A fairly new arrival, name of Cariad Baillie." She scratched an eyebrow, wondering how to explain the presence of a journalist on the ship. "I'll tell you more about her once you've been formerly introduced."

"Mm," Harriet said.

Clio leaned against her desk. "Aravanis is still around

Harriet grinned proudly. "Your first hire! Nice to see your

instincts about her were correct. Have you learned any more about her?"

"First name is Penelope," Clio said, rubbing the back of her hand along her jawline. "Don't know if we found that out before or after we lost you. She, ah... enjoys..." She laughed and shook her head. "No. Not a damn thing."

Harriet laughed and shook her head. She looked around the cabin. "Christ, it's strange. You've made it your own. But there's still so much of me here. So much... familiar."

"I couldn't erase you, Harriet," Clio said, staring at her feet. "I couldn't do this alone. Wouldn't have wanted to try. You were with me, always."

Harriet was silent after that. "I wish..." She made a frustrated sound. "To me, it's been less than a day since I was last here. I haven't had a chance to miss you."

"I understand. I do. And... *you* have to understand that it's been eight years for me. I've mourned you. The scars..." She gestured vaguely at her chest, then wrinkled her nose and dropped her hand. "I can't let myself believe this is real. Not yet."

Harriet nodded. "That's fair."

The silence between them grew until it felt like a hard surface, something they would soon need to physically break in order to move on. Clio decided to shatter it.

"There, ah, is... one more... new name on board you should know about."

"Mm-hmm?"

"Alice Malyns."

Harriet's eyes widened. She sat up straighter and Clio could see her shoulders rise and fall with quickened breath. Clio held her stare, refusing to say anything else before Harriet responded to the stone she'd dropped.

"So you remembered."

"So you *did* know," Clio said.

Harriet looked away.

"For nearly the entire time we knew each other. You knew my name. You knew who I... *what* I was. And you kept that from me."

"Would you have wanted to know?" Harriet asked.

"Me? Clio Landau, the woman who has spent thirty years at sea, and eight years captaining a ship with a crew I'd give my life for? Absolutely not. I wish I could have gone to my grave ignorant of the things I'd done before we met. But back then... when I was a frightened, confused child~"

"...you were over thirty..."

"~desperate for *anything* to hold onto. You had no right to keep it from me. You decided you objected to who I was, what I did, and you kept that information from me."

Harriet chewed her bottom lip and shook her head.

"When did you learn the truth? How long after my accident?"

"A month."

Clio bit back a curse. She'd known it was early, but that was unbelievable. "How did... how did you find out?"

Harriet cleared her throat. Her eyes were shining with unshed tears, and she shifted uncomfortably on the cushion.

"We stopped in London to load up on supplies. We had that girl in those days, Rosetta. She could draw. So we had her make a picture of you that we could show around, ask people if they recognized you. We only had to try a couple of taverns before someone started following us. Ranzi sensed them following and led them into a bottleneck. We tussled a bit and eventually got the upper hand. They said if we knew where we could find 'the butcher,' we owed it to every pirate to slit her throat. They started telling us stories. Things Malyns had done. People she had turned in. She didn't care about who got in her way. She killed crew, innocents, anyone that got between her and a target was fair game.

"I went back to the ship planning to tell you what we'd learned. Honest, I intended to tell you everything, Clio. But as soon as I saw you..." A tear slipped free when she shook her head. "I couldn't walk up to this sweet, innocent girl I had just met and tell her she was a monster. You looked at me. You smiled like I was the most welcome sight in the world. And I was supposed to break you? The right thing in that moment would have been to tell that terrified girl that she was only there to murder us? I couldn't do it, Clio. And I don't regret keeping it from you."

Clio took a deep breath and closed her eyes. "No one has ever recognized me. Not in thirty years. But you found me in a month of showing my picture around."

"Well, you looked different." Harriet looked up. "Do... you not remember?"

Clio opened her eyes and stared at her. "What?"

"I suppose that period was so hectic and full of new information that... it would all blend together. People can't remember being a toddler, so maybe... maybe this is the same thing…"

"What are you talking about?"

Harriet said, "Your hair was auburn when we met. The same color as wet lumber. And it was long, curled at the temples and bound together in a long tail that you wore down your back. You were also more… plump. Your face was rounder, and you had a softness around your corners. When I learned how many people would want you dead, I thought it would be best to… hide you."

Clio tightened her jaw. "What did you do?"

"Cut your hair. It was your decision. I can't believe you don't remember this, Clio. We spoke about how much easier it would be to maintain if it was shorter. So you…" She mimed cutting. "We used lime to bleach it. You liked the way it looked, obviously."

Clio self-consciously touched her hair. "And my face?"

Harriet shrugged. "Took care of itself, actually. A combination of rationing the food we had aboard, plus honest work on a ship… you trimmed down quick. Those cheekbones made you look like a completely different person. You *were* a different person by then."

"I still…" She grunted and pushed away from the desk. "Damn it, Harriet. I… I don't regret the life I've lived. The life *we* made together. I wouldn't trade that for anything. But you took the choice away from me! At that point, when you were my whole world, I like to believe I would have made the right decision. I would never have been the beast you described. But knowing… I could have had my own name."

Harriet stood. "I'm sorry, Clio. But you made your own name. Carved your own path through this world. You didn't have the burden of guilt for the things Alice Malyns did. I like to think I gave you freedom to be your true self. But I understand that perspective is… very self-serving. It makes me a hero in your story, when I may well be the villain."

Clio moved closer to her. "No. No, I… can't hold you responsible for what might have been. Knowing the truth, even hearing my name back then might have triggered something. It could have killed me, this version of me, from ever truly existing. I won't be angry at you for that. But I do need to live with it for a while. I only brought it up because when I learned the truth, I hated you for a few days. For knowing and never telling me. Thirty years, Hare. The one question I was constantly asking, and you knew. Even if the answer was horrific, you *knew*."

Harriet averted her gaze.

Clio touched her cheek, ignoring the stubble she felt under her fingertips. "And you still chose to be with me. That is why I stopped being angry with you. Because you knew what I'd done. Who I was. And you chose me anyway."

Harriet met Clio's eyes. "Clio. Darling. I never had a choice when it came to falling for you."

Clio smiled. "It's bizarre. The voice is so very different. But it's you. I'd know it anywhere. And when I look into your eyes..."

Harriet let the silence carry for a moment, then took a step back. "But it's not."

"No," Clio said, also stepping away.

Harriet went back to the couch and sat down. "It's difficult on my end as well. Imagine clothes that are both too tight and too large. Fastened wrong. Baggy in the wrong places and tight where it shouldn't be. And it's your entire body." She touched her face. "He doesn't even see right. I don't think he needs glasses... and his mouth!" She lowered her jaw and stuck her tongue out. "It's... wide. Too wide. And I keep being afraid I'll bite my tongue."

"We'll figure something out," Clio said.

"I know." Harriet looked around the cabin. "The stone. Is it... I don't know if I even want to see it. But is it here?"

Clio nodded toward the curtain that led to her bedroom. "In there, in the bedside drawer."

"Okay. It's just good to know it's there. If things become too dire, I suppose we can try to find a way to put me back in—"

"No!" Clio snapped.

Harriet jumped at the outburst, then shook her head. "Love, I can't remain in Santiago's body. It would be like killing someone to save my own life."

"Something we've all done from time to time."

Harriet gave her a scolding look. "Killing an *innocent* person, then."

"Mm."

Clio wrapped her arms around herself and moved closer to the divan. After a moment of internal debate, she sat down next to the man who moved and acted so much like her long-lost wife. She tightened her hands into fists, then relaxed one and held it out. Harriet looked at it, then offered her own.

They linked fingers.

"Whatever happens," Clio said softly, "I am incredibly grateful we have this time together. I have missed you so very much, Harriet.

There have been things I wanted to tell you, questions I've been desperate to ask. There have been nights I've lain awake having conversations with the darkness trying to imagine what you would say in reply. But most of all I wanted to say thank you. For making me a better captain. For giving your life to save mine. There have been so many times over the years I haven't felt worthy of that sacrifice, and trying to live up to it has made me a better leader."

Harriet brought Clio's hand to her lips and kissed the knuckles.

"We'll figure out some way to fix this. To make it permanent. I survived losing you once, and I'm not sure I could go through it again. Not by choice."

"I have faith. You've kept my ship sailing for eight years, and the crew seems stronger than ever from what I've seen. And from what Santy remembers." She smiled at the strangeness of that statement. "If anyone can figure out how to keep me around, it's the crew of the *Banshee*."

"I concur. But for now, let's sit here and pretend everything is normal. Would that be okay?"

Harriet smiled. "That would be perfect, love."

Clio shivered to hear that word, in that tone, after so very long. She looked away.

It wasn't real. It couldn't be real, she couldn't let herself believe it was real. Not yet.

No matter how real it might seem at that moment.

CHAPTER FIVE

RANZI WAS already waiting at the dock when Fausta and Cariad finished gathering information at the tavern. Cariad's journal pages were full of bizarre stories about the alleged witch, most of which couldn't possibly be true. It was sad to think of how all these people had chosen to create a mythology around this poor marooned woman instead of trying to help her. They had retrieved Estacia from the room where they'd left her. Now they were taking what they'd learned back to the *Banshee* where hopefully this whole mess would be explained.

To her surprise, she didn't have to wait long. Fausta placed herself in the bow of the launch and, as soon as they were underway, snapped her fingers to get everyone's attention.

"You need to know what's waiting for us on the ship." She wet her lips and narrowed her eyes, trying to think of how to phrase it. "The witch, Granny Wise, was apparently very powerful. She could grant wishes, your greatest desires. But it came at a cost. Sometimes, it would seem, the cost was your soul, a debt paid upon death."

Cariad nodded and tapped her journal. "Several people mentioned that. You lived your life, no deadlines or anything like that where the Devil comes claiming after a set number of years. But once you died, your soul was captured in a stone."

Fausta nodded. "That's right. And apparently it's true. It seems Captain Landau... ah, the *first* Captain Landau, Harriet... made a deal with Granny Wise 'fore she set out on a life of piracy. So when she died, Granny Wise got her soul. It went into a stone. And when Granny Wise died, Santiago Zeno got his hands on the stone. It had a design on it that he recognized. Harriet's tattoo. So he saved it, gave it to Clio as a... a memento."

Estacia said, "That was sweet of him."

"Hm," Fausta grunted. "And then something... happened. Don't ask me what, or how the fuck any of it works. But apparently it got out."

"What got out?" Cariad asked.

"Harriet's soul."

Ranzi wrinkled her brow. "Out of the stone?"

"And went into Santiago."

Ranzi stopped rowing. The launch, now silent, bobbed on the water as she stared at Fausta. "What does that mean?"

Fausta said, "It means that as near as I can tell, Harriet Landau's soul has taken control of Santiago's body. I wouldn't have believed it, either. But if you had *seen* him... He moves different. He talks different. The tattoo that was on Harriet's arm appeared on his, out of nowhere. It just... it appeared. I'm sure they've found out more while I was on the island with you lot. But I could see it in Clio's eyes before I left. She believed it. And if she was convinced..."

Cariad said, "That's not possible."

"You don't believe in the soul?" Estacia asked.

"It's not about that. Whether it exists or not, it can't~ it wouldn't be able to..." She looked down at her journal, thinking about some of the stories she'd heard about Granny Wise. She shook her head. They couldn't be true, and neither could what Fausta was telling them now. "A stone? For eight years? A-and even if *that* much was possible, there isn't any way it could possess someone else's body."

"After everything we've seen," Ranzi said, "I don't know that I'd doubt it. You were here for the island that was only visible to those who were looking for it. Everything about that job was unnatural and peculiar. What's different about this?"

"This is about the *soul*," Cariad said. "It can't be bartered or used as a bargaining chip. And it certainly can't be stored on a shelf like a jar of plums." She looked at Fausta. "This man, Santiago, he must be lying. Playing on Captain Landau's emotions for some sort of scheme."

Fausta shrugged. "It's a possibility. Although that seems about as unbelievable as Harriet's soul surviving in a rock. They've been friends for ages. This would be a cruel lie, and I can't imagine any treasure worth being so hurtful. I just wanted you to be prepared for what we were walking into when we got back." She looked at Ranzi. "And the sooner the better, hm?"

Ranzi nodded and went back to rowing.

Cariad looked at Estacia, then looked past Fausta at the *Banshee*, hoping that a swindler lurked on the deck waiting to prey on their captain's loneliness.

It was a terrible thing to hope for, but the alternate was so much worse that she couldn't even bear to imagine it.

Aboard the ship, the group went immediately to Clio's cabin. The captain was at her desk, and a man Cariad had never seen before was lying on her divan. He looked disheveled and shaken as if he had just come through a storm. Clio didn't look much better. She stood up when Ranzi opened the door, hope flooding into her eyes as she saw them all. The man she assumed to be Santiago Zeno sat up but kept his arms wrapped protectively around himself.

"What did you find?" Clio asked.

Fausta and Ranzi stepped to either side, and Cariad realized she had the floor. She cleared her throat and stepped forward. "Okay. Well, um..."

"Wait, who is this?" Santiago asked.

Cariad looked at him, then at Clio. "I'm Cariad Baillie. I-I'm... I haven't been on the crew very long."

"What do you do here?" the man asked. "You look like a librarian."

Ranzi smirked. "Not far off."

Cariad raised her eyebrows. She'd never met Santiago or Harriet, so she had nothing to compare the man to. She cleared her throat and nervously touched her glasses.

"I'm a journalist."

Santiago - or rather, Harriet - raised her eyebrows. "A journalist? On the *Banshee*?" She got to her feet and turned to Clio. "Why is a journalist on my ship?"

Ranzi sucked in a breath through her teeth, then shook her head. "My God," she said under her breath. "That *is* Harriet."

Clio bristled. "It's *my* ship, actually. And we have our reasons for inviting her aboard. The most pertinent being that she makes herself useful. Go ahead, Cariad."

Cariad cleared her throat. She glanced sideways at Harriet, then opened her journal.

"It-it seems as if Granny Wise is the source of many legends and rumors around the island. It's difficult to separate the truth from the lies. Until I knew about..." She gestured at Harriet without looking at her. "I assumed most of the unbelievable things were just embellishments. But now I'm not so sure. Residents left offerings for her on the weekend. Food, drink, baubles, whatever they could spare. If they didn't please her, they believed she would retaliate with storms, shipwrecks, the British Navy. Basically any bad luck was attributed to making her angry. So they appeased her."

Fausta said, "A lot of people were upset we were even asking questions, even though most of them believe the body pulled out of the forest was hers."

"Ah, I may know why. They believe the body was hers, but they don't believe she's dead. I didn't know about... the... stones... and souls. So I dismissed it. But I wrote it down. They think she's been alive for four hundred years. She survives by jumping from an old, dying body to a younger one. So they were scared because they think she's still out there somewhere."

Clio looked at Harriet. "Can you... ah... d-does Santiago know if that's a possibility?"

Harriet seemed to think for a moment. "He's heard the rumor before. People who sought Granny Wise sometimes went missing. She could have taken their bodies and then buried the corpse where no one would find it. Travelers have been sparse lately, he says. She might have succumbed before she could find an appropriate vessel to steal."

Ranzi lifted an eyebrow. "You think a woman who can pop souls in and out of a body would ever let that happen? There's a whole town full of people just down the path. More coming in every day. Even if people weren't specifically seeking her out, I can't imagine she'd just lay down and die without a fight."

Harriet sat up straighter. "Maybe she didn't. There... there was a ship." She stood up and jabbed her finger at the air. "About two weeks before the body showed up in the forest, a ship was forced to stay in the harbor an extra day because their captain's wife went missing. She was gone an entire day. Santiago says they were readying a search party. Then she just came strolling down the main road. Didn't have a mark on her, said she didn't remember where she'd been or what had happened. Her husband was positive someone had taken advantage of her, but she convinced him she was fine."

"What ship?" Fausta asked at the same time Clio asked, "What captain?"

Harriet blinked in surprise. "The *Loyal Sea*. Captain John Ronan. We know him."

Clio was also surprised. "Right. He's a privateer. Legitimate and commissioned." She remembered the one conversation she'd had with him. It had not been her best day... "He's a good man."

Ranzi said, "Might want to steer fair clear, then. Good men are bad business for folks like us."

Harriet shook her head. "Actually we shouldn't have to worry about him. We've crossed paths enough times. He knew who we were, but respected us enough to turn a blind eye as long as we kept ourselves mostly moral. We can approach under a flag of truce. I think once he hears what we have to say, he'll be more than willing to grant us leave."

Ranzi looked skeptical but didn't argue.

To Harriet, Clio said, "Does Santiago have any idea where Ronan's ship was headed when they left here?"

"The quartermaster said something about being late to a contract in Cyprus. But it's been months. There's no chance they'd still be there now."

Fausta was already heading for the door. "Still, it should be easy enough to find them from there, if we get moving now." She paused at the doorway and turned back to look at Clio.

"Go, tell Aravanis to set course."

Fausta nodded and left.

Cariad said, "Do you really believe this Granny Wise person stole the body of Captain Ronan's wife? And even if that was possible, and even if she did it, why would she leave the island?" She held up her journal. "These people say she's been operating here for hundreds of years. What would make her leave now?"

"I don't particularly care, Miss Baillie," Clio said. "I only care if this witch is still alive. Because if she is, she'll know how we can get Santiago's body back to him, and find a permanent way to give Harriet back to us. That's worth tracking them down for."

Aravanis reported it would take them four days at full sail to reach Cyprus. Once they were underway, Fausta took Harriet back to her cabin to retrieve the discarded clothes she'd left behind after her 'awakening.' The idea of slipping back into Santiago's unwashed outfit was nauseating, but it was better than strolling around in a sheet. Fausta remained by the door while Harriet gathered her host's shirt and pants, then took a seat on the bed to dress.

"So you all agreed to have the journalist on board?" she asked. "You trust her?"

"As much as you can trust someone who shares secrets for a living," Fausta said. "She's never done anything to make us question her."

Harriet grunted noncommittally.

"She wrote a book about us. The crew. About how we all came to be aboard the ship. The captain was worried it might give away too much about us. Lead the Navy to come crashing down on our heads. But when she finished writing it, she came back aboard and gave Clio the only copy. Said she could do whatever she wanted with it. As far as I know, it's still locked away in her cabin."

"I suppose that's something." She sniffed the shirt and grunted. "If this situation isn't remedied soon, I may choose to go back into the stone. There's something to be said for being insensate."

"Sorry about that. The ship still doesn't have much need for male clothing. I'll ask around some of the deckhands. Maybe one of the powder monkeys has something."

"I'd appreciate it." She sighed and stood up, tugging at the material of her shirt. "Is she fitting in well with everyone? The... writer." She sneered the word like it was a slur.

Fausta said, "I like her well enough. She seems to have bonded with a few of us." She smirked. "Estacia, mostly."

"Really?" Harriet chuckled. "Well, that's something, at least. I'm glad to hear she's getting some excitement in her life."

"No question about that."

Fausta looked her up and down. "Whatever it might feel like, you make it look good."

Harriet chuckled nervously. "I'm still a little foggy about the first few seconds after I, ah, woke up like this. But it seems pretty clear what was happening in here. I don't know if I should apologize or~"

"Don't waste too much time thinking on it," Fausta said. "Plenty of other things to occupy our thoughts. And since Santiago is in there listening in.. it was a lovely distraction on an afternoon, and I thank him very much for his service."

Harriet chuckled. "Don't ask me how I know this or how it would even be possible, but I think somehow he's blushing."

Fausta nodded, smiling. "I have that effect on men."

They returned to the deck. This time Harriet didn't flinch when she entered the sunlight, but she did hold a hand above her eyes to shield them. She was almost certain there was something wrong with Santiago's eyes, but he seemed to have found a way to deal with it. She walked to the railing and leaned against it, looking out over the water as the ship started its eastward journey.

Fausta joined her. "How about you, Captain? The way you're looking at it, you just cheated death and then jumped almost a decade into the future. Your ship is still here, but someone else is giving orders. Sure, it's your wife, but..."

"It's very odd," Harriet admitted. "I held out hope for some miraculous rescue even as they led me onto the gallows. I don't hold it against anyone for not succeeding, to be clear. I know you all would have moved heaven and earth to save me if it had been at all possible. So I didn't quite believe it was the end until the rope was around my neck." She reached up and massaged her throat. "I accepted it. I think accepting it is why I didn't feel any pain. It goes dark before the actual..."

She pressed her lips together and refused to continue the thought.

Fausta said, "I suppose that's a blessing."

"Mm." She half-smiled and looked over at Fausta. "And may I say, I never believed in Heaven, but when the darkness when away and I found myself thrusting on top of a beautiful naked woman, I thought, 'well, I suppose I must have been wrong about that.'"

Fausta laughed. "I'll take that compliment, and thank ye kindly." She looked over her shoulder to make sure no one was close enough to eavesdrop. "Clio has taken a lover or two since you've been gone. I know she's taken Delfina to bed a few times. But those are just... they don't mean..." She looked at Harriet. "Her feelings for you have never changed, or faded, or been given to another."

Harriet looked down into the water. "I don't know if that's lovely or unbearably tragic."

"You're here," Fausta said. "Maybe not in the ideal way, but she got you back. So if you ask me, I think it means her dedication has proven worthwhile. I think it's unbearably romantic."

Harriet considered, and then nodded.

Unbearably romantic did sound right.

CHAPTER SIX

ARAVANIS HAD the helm for most of their journey to Cyprus. The winds were very favorable and carried them well. She kept her eye on the horizon for other ships or hazards they would prefer to avoid. She didn't mind that no one else took a shift. She didn't need much sleep, and steering their ship through calm seas gave her time to explore her inner thoughts.

Everyone else was too distracted to navigate properly, anyway. Their previous captain was back. Harriet Landau. In the body of a man. Aravanis had never known the woman particularly well. She had been recruited by Clio, who at the time had been serving as something of a second-in-command. But she knew Harriet had been a good captain who earned her crew's loyalty by being dedicated to them in return. She'd been there when Harriet died. She knew the captain was only taken prisoner as a ploy to earn her crew a chance to escape. That was the only fact Aravanis needed to know about the woman to trust her. Even if she *was* currently a passenger in someone else's body.

The story about their new male passenger quickly spread across the ship. Harriet kept mostly to herself, sticking close to either Clio, Fausta, or Delfina when she wasn't hidden away in Clio's quarters or the infirmary. As far as Aravanis could tell, she was spending her nights in the infirmary as it seemed like the least awkward choice.

By the time she spotted Cyprus on the horizon, business aboard the ship had mostly returned to normal. The whispers had stopped, and the man called Harriet could cross the deck without catching the eye of every sailor she passed. Clio was still having a hell of a time processing her wife's return, which was to be expected.

Aravanis watched as the captain stepped out from below deck, saw Harriet at the railing, and cut hard to the left. She came to the quarterdeck and examined the compass, then looked out ahead of them.

"We're making good time," she said.

"Aye."

Aravanis kept her eyes forward and kept their ship steady. She knew that if the captain wanted to talk, she would have gone to literally anyone else on the ship first.

When the captain remained at her side, Aravanis took a step back from the helm. "Would you like to take over for the last leg?"

Clio started to refuse, then understood what she was being asked. It would give her something to do, keep her busy, give her an excuse to avoid the crew and the questions they were certain to have.

"Yes, I would. Thank you."

Aravanis nodded and gave up her position. Clio took her place and turned to catch her eye. She gave the captain a single nod, which was more than enough to encompass a full conversation. Clio smiled gratefully and then faced forward again.

Aravanis went down to the deck. Harriet saw her coming and stepped away from the rail. Aravanis tensed but didn't change her course. After a few steps, the woman was walking beside her.

"You're the bo's'n, right? Artemis?"

"Aravanis. We met."

"Right. Sorry. I'm still getting used to all these new people on my... on *the* ship. The memories of my last day, the last... week or so, to be honest, are a bit fuzzy. But I remember you. You were with me on the... the day we..."

Aravanis nodded. "Yes."

"So I must have trusted you, if you were part of my landing party. If you're not busy, I was hoping we could talk. I want to know what's happened aboard since I... since..." She cleared her throat and grimaced. "The others I could ask, I'm afraid they won't be able to stop seeing me as their former captain and as Clio's wife. They might embellish things to make her look better, or to make me feel like I'm missed. I want the truth. And you seem like the best chance to get an unbiased truth."

She stopped and looked out at the water. "There's a writer onboard. Baillie. She didn't serve under you. She would be impartial."

Harriet wrinkled her nose. "I was hoping to avoid talking to her. I'm not a fan of journalists. I don't much like the fact she's aboard, if I'm honest."

Aravanis took a deep breath and let it out. She still hadn't looked away from the water. "I don't like talking. You won't get much of a story from me. The journalist is your best hope for what you want."

She turned and left Harriet behind in the sunlight.

She didn't know why she was reacting so harshly to the ghost. Although perhaps it was that simple. Harriet Landau was dead, her body given to the sea. Rituals had been performed, and those who loved her had mourned, grieved, healed. For her to be back like this was unnatural. Aravanis had seen plenty of inexplicable and supernatural things since she first set foot on a sailing ship. Hell, her own life had been saved because the ship passed through a mystical barrier around a magic island. She was accustomed to arcane and otherworldly things.

But that didn't mean she had to sit down and have a conversation with it.

Harriet, via Santiago's knowledge, told them Ronan had most likely headed to a port town on the south-east side of the island called Skala. When they docked, Fausta went ashore with Ranzi, Aravanis, and Cariad to see what they could learn about the current whereabouts of the *Loyal Sea*. Their first stop was the sprawling shack at the end of the main pier. The dockmaster had come outside to greet them, eyeing the ship. He was low to the ground and wide enough to look like he was part of the landscape. His cheeks were chubby but mostly hidden behind a silver beard. He waited to speak until they were close enough to speak without raising their voices.

"Manner of business?" he said.

"Looking for a friend at the moment," Fausta said. "Our ship is freelance transportation. Goods, livestock, and passengers. We've got open space if you know of anyone looking."

He grunted and handed over the paperwork to acknowledge their arrival in port. As she signed, she looked past him and tried to affect a casual tone.

"Our friend is sailing aboard the *Loyal Sea*. Rumor is they passed through here a month back, maybe two. You wouldn't happen to know where they went from here, would you?"

He grabbed the pen and paper back from her. "You'll be forgetting that friend if you know what's good for you."

Fausta frowned. The reason she had come right out and asked was because Captain Ronan was a privateer. He was free and legal, commissioned to sail the *Loyal Sea* under the umbrella of the Royal Navy. An official ship like that was no cause for this kind of vitriol.

"What happened?" she asked. "Did they capture the wrong ship or something?"

The dockmaster grunted again. "Went rogue. Came here like you said, but they were only here to supply themselves. Raided the tavern. Barkeep tried to stop 'em, led to a whole scuffle. They took all the bottles they didn't break in the fight. Also got the armory, the larder. We put up a helluva fight when they got to the treasury, so they didn't get the payroll. But they damn sure tried, and they took a pound of flesh instead before they finally fell back to the ship."

Fausta and Ranzi exchanged looks. Fausta didn't know John Ronan particularly well, but this didn't sound remotely close to someone Clio would consider an associate. Cariad was looking at the town and Fausta turned to do the same. The quiet hadn't seemed suspicious when they arrived, but now she couldn't help finding it eerie.

"I was hoping you were a relief ship," the dockmaster said.

Ranzi said, "We may be able to part with a few things. I'll have to ask our cook about the food situation. We've been lucky."

"Any little bit would help. It's been lean weeks since Ronan's blasted ship came through."

"We'll go back now," Fausta said. "We'll tell the captain about your situation and see what we can do to ease your woes. In exchange, can you ask around and see if anyone knows where the *Loyal Sea* went next?"

He narrowed his eyes. "I hope you don't consider them friends after what they done."

"Definitely not," she assured him. "But part of helping you involves stopping them, if it's within our power."

He considered that. Then he nodded. "I'll ask around."

"It's much appreciated."

Fausta motioned for the others to follow her back to the launch. Cariad watched the dockmaster as he waddled off, then hurried to catch up with the group.

"Why would privateers suddenly go rogue like that?"

"It's not unheard of," Ranzi said. "Frustration with the top brass, greed, boredom. A good number of privateers decide to rip up their commissions. That said, I can't help but think the timing of this is strange." Aravanis pushed away from the pier and began rowing. "Fausta, what do we know so far about Granny Wise and her movements?"

Fausta held up a hand, counting off each incident. "The *Loyal Sea* visited Islas Baleares a few months ago. The captain's wife disappeared for an uncertain amount of time, then magically reappeared, apparently none the worse for wear. We don't know what happened during the four or five days it took them to get from there to Cyprus, but apparently something bad enough occurred to make Captain Ronan turn pirate."

"You're assuming it was him," Cariad said. "You missed the fact that Granny Wise supposedly hopped from body to body in order to grant herself immortality. Her body was found after the *Loyal Sea* left Baleares. We can at least entertain the theory that Granny Wise took over... do we know the name of Captain Ronan's wife?"

"Priscilla... Penelope... Puh-peh..." Ranzi narrowed her eyes, then snapped her fingers. "Isobel."

"Granny Wise took over Isobel Ronan's body."

"And used it to leave Baleares for the first time in four hundred years?" Ranzi said. "Why? If she'd really been pulling this scam for so long, why did she suddenly feel the need to jump on a ship and convince them to turn pirate?"

Cariad shook her head. "It's confusing. But she must have had a reason. The easiest way to figure out what it might be is to just ask her."

Fausta started to say something, then stopped herself. Cariad caught it, though, and said, "What? You disagree?"

"I don't disagree, no," Fausta said. "But I wonder if it's smart to pursue her as enemies. We need her help to figure out what to do with Harriet."

Cariad said, "We can't turn a blind eye to what they did on

Skala."

"And we won't," Fausta said. "But we need to help Harriet first. If that means pretending like we don't know or care about what they did to those people, then that may be what we have to do. I don't like the idea any more than you do. Either way, it won't be your decision, nor mine."

She looked to the *Banshee*. Clio would be the one who set the tone of their pursuit.

Fausta didn't envy her the choice that would have to be made.

Harriet was at the farthest table in the mess, utilizing the shadows that gathered there to keep anyone else who wandered into the room from noticing her. She had retrieved Santiago's bag, the one he'd brought with him aboard the ship, and emptied out the stones within. Her own stone, the one she apparently spent the past decade occupying, was still in Clio's quarters. The others were now spread out in front of Harriet on the table. She picked them up at random to feel their weight, to examine the designs etched into the surfaces.

Eventually she was the only person in the mess. Estacia came out from the larder, spotted Harriet in the corner, and made her way over. She stopped a few steps away.

"Would you prefer to be left alone?"

"When the alternative is time with you, never." Harriet gestured at the bench across from her. "I'm just thinking about these stones. The people who made deals that resulted in them being created." She picked up a stone at random. It was ringed with triangles that it took Harriet a moment to translate as waves. "How many of these deals are complete? How many souls were in that bag with me? And what happens to them now if Granny Wise is truly gone?"

Estacia picked up one of the stones. "Some of them may be out there right now. What was she doing with them?"

"She said she used them to see the world. To experience things she would otherwise never get close to. That's why she made the deal with me. She wanted to be a pirate." She looked at the other stones. "I wonder what these other people are. What she gave them."

"Mm." Estacia put the stone back. "People have all kinds of wishes."

Harriet cleared her throat. "I want to make sure people know.

So that, if the time comes, it's not just coming from one person. If we don't find Granny Wise, or if there's no way to find a way to bring me back permanently, I don't want to stay like this. This is Santiago's body and I have no right to it. It's bad enough that I've hijacked it this long already. I will not do it permanently, even if it means I have to die or go back into the stone. I don't know what might happen. If Clio is forced to make a decision in a split second, I don't want people to think she was being cruel or choosing a relative stranger over me."

"I understand." Estacia put her hand on top of Harriet's. "And I want *you* to know that even if it's strange, it is very nice to have your presence on the ship again. We've missed you."

Harriet smiled. "It's good to know the ship has thrived in my absence. The best part of giving up your life for people is knowing your sacrifice wasn't in vain."

Estacia nodded. "And Clio is a very good captain."

"That's comforting to know. She was basically doing the job with me toward the end anyway, so I'm not surprised. Sometimes I worried about... if she would be okay without me." She cocked her head to the side and laughed softly. "I don't know if I'm relieved or hurt to know that she's done so remarkably well."

"She's using what you taught her. You should take comfort in that, and just let everything else go."

"I think that's good advice. Although I'm not sure I can trust your judgement." She aimed a finger at Estacia. "I turn my back for a few years, and you start servicing journalists?"

Estacia laughed. "I was a jerk to her when we met and I felt bad. So then I tried to be overly nice to her to make up for it. And that... got out of hand."

Harriet grinned. She raised her cup. "Well, apparently it's been going on for months, so I'm happy you're happy."

"I'm overjoyed." She didn't have a cup of her own, so she knocked her knuckle against the side of Harriet's. "In fact, when we got word that you'd come back, we were right in the middle of~"

Ranzi interrupted by coming into the mess at a fast trot. Estacia twisted on the bench to face her.

"Estacia. How are we doing on food stores?"

"We're good. Why?"

"We may need to send some to the island. Skala needs supplies."

Estacia was already rising from her seat. "Yes, yeah, of course."

Ranzi said, "Harriet, come topside. There's been a development."

"Developments." Harriet sighed and dropped her cup back to the table and stood up. "That's rarely a good thing to hear at times like this."

Estacia raised an eyebrow and crossed her fingers.

Harriet leaned down next to Estacia as she passed her. "If I'm still around when this is all over, I want to know what I interrupted."

Estacia chuckled. "Promise."

Ranzi and Harriet left, and Estacia went to the larder to see if she could make good on her promise.

Chapter Seven

THE BANSHEE soared across the water. They were headed north, to the Aegean, the last known destination of Captain Ronan and the *Loyal Sea*. Clio was in her cabin, arms crossed so she could clasp her elbows in the opposite hands, a self-embrace that was helping her process the past few days. They had given the people of Skala what they could spare without creating scarcity for themselves, and she feared it still hadn't been close to enough. Those people were suffering, and she couldn't for the life of her imagine what would have made Ronan change so drastically.

She didn't know him well, but their paths had crossed twice over the years. The first time occurred when she was still just a member of Harriet's crew. She was coming to terms with the fact she had no memory and no past, still clinging to her future wife's belt like a stray kitten. They had been hired for what they believed to be a legitimate hauling job that required picking up cargo from a port in Spain and hauling it to a small Greek island.

When they arrived, the *Loyal Sea* cut them off. After a little saber-rattling, Harriet realized Ronan wasn't acting like someone trying to steal the loot out from under them. "He's *defending* it," she said. So she raised the white flag and asked for parlay. Ronan explained the men who hired the *Banshee* weren't the rightful owners of the cargo and had no right to sell it. He had been recruited to defend it from whoever showed up.

"The sellers expected we would just assume he was a thief, fight him off, and go about the job," Harriet explained to the crew later. "We're lucky Ronan was willing to listen to reason."

They had parted on good terms, with the job abandoned. Harriet kept the original fee, "for our trouble." She told Ronan where to find the men who had hired them and wished him luck dealing with them.

Clio had remembered the interaction years later, not long after Harriet's death. They'd happened to be docked near the *Loyal Sea* in London. Clio was still mourning her wife, barely aware of what day it was, and she'd only left the ship that day because Delfina insisted upon it. "You need to feel the earth beneath your feet, if just to remember how solid it feels."

Clio went directly to a tavern, where she proceeded to drink so much that the earth didn't feel particularly solid at all. In fact, it was quite a bit wilder than the waves once she had a few drinks in her. She'd ventured into the alley to purge what she'd spent the morning drinking and rested her forehead against the bricks as she caught her breath.

She was almost passed out when a heavy hand landed on her shoulder. She startled and reached for a weapon. Even before she remembered she'd left her knives and guns on the ship, the owner of the hand was already speaking in a calming voice.

"Relax. It's okay. I'm watching your back."

She turned to see a man she didn't recognize, but would eventually discover to be John Ronan. She wiped her sleeve across her mouth and turned so she could rest her shoulders against the wall.

"I don't need your protection."

"You're unarmed, alone, and you've been spilling bills and coins out of your pocket every time you paid for a drink. There are at least five men in there who have been waiting for an opportunity to pounce and take whatever you have left. Do you think you could fight them off in your condition?"

She spit on the ground between her feet. "Let them come."

He said, "You're Clio Landau, correct?"

She looked up at him.

"I knew your wife. Briefly."

Clio bristled. Very few people referred to Harriet as her wife.

Co-captain, partner, other code words that allowed them to pretend their relationship was something that didn't challenge their small view of the world. To hear this man use the word so casually cut through some of her drunken haze.

"She was a good woman," he continued. "Honorable. And I don't use that word lightly, especially not to describe a pirate. But she earned the respect. I didn't think much of a ship crewed by women. I heard stories about how she treated her people." He sighed softly. "I was very sorry to hear of her passing. But it was a truly heroic death, despite the circumstances."

"Fuck that," Clio snapped. "You don't believe that. She was a pirate. A thief and a criminal, and she was executed for breaking the law." She sneered at him. "You probably think it was *justice.*"

Ronan took a moment to compose his response, head down and lips pursed. "Her job was her job, whether or not I approve of it. People make all kinds of choices that take them down their paths. If I'd had her life, maybe I'd have ended up in the same place. So I work hard not to judge on that count. The only thing that truly matters is her choice in the moment. To give up her own life so that her crew could survive. It was selfless. I can honor that, no matter who she was."

Clio grunted. "I don't care if it was the most heroic death in history. It was fucking selfish. Taking herself away from me like that."

He smiled sadly. "I understand that, too."

Clio's stomach roiled again and she pitched forward. Ronan put a hand on her back. She breathed deeply a few times until the nausea passed, then straightened up again.

"Don't leave the bar alone," he said. "Promise me that. I don't trust your safety getting back to your ship like this."

"I can handle a drunk asshole who preys on other drunk assholes."

"Yes, but you can't handle five of them at once if they decide to team up. Just promise me, okay? You'll find me and let me escort you back to the docks when you're ready."

She waved her hand, grunting an affirmation.

"Good. It was good to meet you, Captain."

Clio closed her eyes and took a few more steadying breaths. When she opened them again, her mysterious defender was still standing beside her. She sighed and pushed away from the wall. Her legs wobbled beneath her but she managed to stand without leaning on him.

"Fine. Might as well go now."

He had walked her back to the ship. There had been times since when she wondered if he had saved her life that night. No one had accosted them on the walk, but was that because he was such an imposing figure? It was hard to say. He'd delivered her to the *Banshee* and stayed long enough to let Delfina know how much she'd had to drink - the traitor - and then disappeared back to shore.

After that, she'd always kept an ear open for news of Ronan and the *Loyal Sea*. Sometimes they were docked near each other, other times she would see him sailing away from an island just as the *Banshee* approached. She'd never had another conversation with the man, and she had always regretted that. She'd wanted to thank him for his kindness that night, for using the word 'wife' when so many refused. She'd always wondered if he had stories about Harriet that she'd never heard.

And now *he* was the vicious pirate. His crew had ravaged a town and left them gasping for air. She couldn't imagine that steely-eyed man in his crisp uniform doing something so cruel and inhumane. Granny Wise must have been responsible, but how? Had she granted the deepest, darkest desire of someone on the crew? Had Ronan always secretly wanted to be freed from the burden of conscience?

Her cabin door opened, followed by a soft, "Shit," and then a knock. "I'm sorry," Harriet said. "It's been over a week, I should be out of the habit by now. This isn't my cabin anymore."

Clio waved her in. "It's always been your cabin, as far as I'm concerned. And it always will be."

Harriet closed the door behind her. "I daresay you've earned it. But I won't complain about still being welcomed in your private space."

Clio couldn't resist a smile, but it faded when she looked toward the window again. "I don't know what's going to happen when we catch up with Ronan. We must confront him about what his crew did at Skala. And if he's doing it to other towns, we should stop him. And then he's supposed to believe us that his wife is possessed by an immortal witch?" She laughed and rubbed her forehead. "A witch we then have to ask for a favor to get you... to..."

"Yes," Harriet said, "that's a sticking point for me as well. If we *do* find Granny Wise, what exactly are we asking her to do? I accept the fact my body is long gone. And I refuse to take someone else's body. So where does that leave us?"

"I've been thinking about that." She turned to face Harriet. "Santiago is... present, correct?"

Harriet nodded. "He's there."

"So if the original soul remains, then someone could volunteer-"

"I'm not taking your body, love."

Clio pressed her lips together. "Why not? It's what I want. It's..."

Harriet came around the desk and cupped Clio's face in her hands. "Stop this. I remember this from when we first found each other. When you were lost and confused. You felt you were expendable, that you weren't allowed to exist. I won't have you go back to thinking that way. You've come too far for it. You've made a name for yourself. A life for yourself. This is *your* crew now, not mine."

Clio closed her eyes. She turned her head and kissed Harriet's palm. "I wouldn't care. As long as I had you back."

"I know, love."

Clio stepped forward, her eyes still closed, and pressed her lips to Harriet's. For a moment, the kiss was exactly as she remembered. The lips were soft. They yielded to hers, and Harriet returned the kiss with passion. Clio moaned softly as she sank into a feeling she'd been aching for so long that she'd forgotten what relief felt like. She wrapped her arms around Harriet's waist, only briefly noting that it was wider than it once was.

The differences didn't matter, because all her mind registered were the similarities. This was how Harriet kissed, that was almost the sound Harriet made, that was the way she took control and guided Clio to the wall. She felt the wood against her back, felt Harriet's rough hand on her breast. The fingers reached much farther than they ever had before.

Then Harriet pressed her body against Clio's, and she felt something she'd never felt before. Alarm bells rang in her mind, and she twisted away from the man's body pinning her to the wall. "Stop," she gasped, turning away from the kiss. She put her hands flat on his stomach and shoved him back. He stumbled over his feet and caught the edge of the desk to keep from falling.

Clio moved to her right to build distance between them, her head still turned away. She wiped at her mouth. She could taste him now, and she resisted the urge to spit by wiping her hand across her mouth. His taste and his smell… it filled the room like smoke.

"I'll go."

"No," Clio said, but her tone was unconvincing. "I wanted that to happen. I-I just…"

Harriet straightened her clothes. "I'll go," she repeated.

Clio finally looked at her again. "I'm sorry, love."

"Don't be." Harriet looked down at herself and held her arms out. "I would have reacted the same way. We'll… figure something out. But for now I think it would be best if I leave."

"Perhaps so," Clio said.

Harriet left.

Clio dropped into her seat and covered her eyes with one hand. She was trembling, both from disappointment and confusion about what she'd almost done.

She didn't know how long she sat there sorting through her emotions before she heard a shout from above. Tis Common, their lookout, had spotted the *Loyal Sea*.

Clio rose quickly and grabbed her cutlass, strapping the sheath to her belt as she stormed from the cabin and raced onto the deck.

At the moment, she didn't care if confronting Ronan led to a fight. Anything was better than sorting out her complicated feelings.

At least in a fight, she could punch things.

"Ready ho!" Fausta bellowed, one hand on the rail of the quarterdeck as she watched the men move to comply with her orders. "Mainsail haul!"

Ranzi was at the helm, keeping them steady as the ship lunged hard off its original course. Her shirt was sleeveless and Fausta was well-impressed by the way the muscles flexed and moved under the other woman's dark skin. But she refused to let herself be distracted, and watched the crew guided their swing.

The massive canvas sails deflated as they lost the wind that had brought them this far. The ship turned hard starboard, changing tack so they could pull up behind the *Loyal Sea* and give chase. The men lifted anchors on some lines, reined in others, and the sails responded to their expert handling until their corners found the breeze. They rippled and whipped until they were in the right spot. The yards were braced and the wind carried them toward their prey.

Clio joined them. She held a hand over her eyes to shield the sun, squinting at the rapidly-growing ship ahead of them.

"Have they seen us yet?"

"They haven't made any attempt to evade us," Ranzi said. "No reason why they should. They're still flying the right colors."

Clio had noticed that. "Odd, don't you think?"

"It's a good disguise," Fausta said. "Up until a few days ago, we thought they were still sailing as commissioned privateers. If they really are raiding ports like Skala, it's a good way to make sure your victims keep their guards down."

"They think we don't know what we're sailing into," Clio said.

"We might want to keep up the illusion of our ignorance, Captain," Ranzi said. "No reason to antagonize them until we know a little more."

Clio nodded. "Makes sense. When we're close enough, signal them that we just want to have a cordial conversation."

"Cordial." Fausta looked at the sword on Clio's hip. "With that?"

"We *are* still a pirate vessel," Clio said.

"Aye," Fausta said with a smile. "That much is true."

Soon they had gained enough distance that they could see the *Loyal Sea*'s crew lined up at their railing, watching their approach. Their arrival seemed to have caused quite a stir, and soon it seemed as if every person aboard the other ship had come to see who their guest was.

Clio went down to their own railing. They were close enough to be heard if she shouted. "Ahoy, *Loyal Sea!*" She scanned the faces for John Ronan. "I am Captain Clio Landau, of the ship *Banshee*. I formally request a peaceful conversation with your captain."

The other crew spoke amongst themselves. One man broke away from the pack and hurried off.

Cariad joined Clio at the railing and looked warily across the gap between their ships. "What's happening now?" she asked under her breath, despite the fact her normal speaking voice wouldn't have traveled the distance to their ears.

"Now we wait to see if he grants us parlay." Clio kept her hands clasped in front of her, impatiently drumming her fingers against her left wrist.

Minutes passed where the only sound was the flapping of sails, the creak of wood, and the occasional slap of water caught between their ships. Clio was about to call for an update when the man who'd run off returned. He shouldered his way to the front of the crowd.

"You," he shouted, pointing at Clio. He held up two fingers. "Two others. No weapons."

"I suppose that's fair." Clio unfastened her cutlass and handed the belt to Ranzi. "You're in command."

Ranzi cleared her throat. "Are you sure on that...?"

Clio raised an eyebrow. "Who else would you suggest?"

Ranzi shrugged. "There just so happens to be another captain aboard, that's all."

"Ah. I suppose that's true..." She pressed her lips together and looked past Ranzi to Harriet, standing on the quarterdeck. "You're in command, Ranzi."

"As you wish."

She also unholstered her gun, removed the dagger from her boot, and fished the brass knuckles from the pocket of her coat. She passed these all to Cariad, who fumbled to hold it without dropping anything.

"Criminy, how many weapons do you have on ya?"

"More than that," Clio said without moving her lips. "But we have to make it look good. Aravanis, Fausta, you're with me."

The *Loyal Sea* extended a bridge, which crewmembers of the *Banshee* anchored on their side. Once it was secure, Clio climbed up and crossed over. Aravanis and Fausta, similarly disarmed, followed behind her in a line.

The same man who'd called across waited until they were all aboard, then motioned for them to follow him. Aravanis brought up the rear, more dangerous unarmed than most of the crew would have been fully armed.

The crewman took them belowdecks to the captain's ready room. He stopped next to the door, clearly intending to remain there as sentry. Clio knocked once and then let herself in.

The ready room was a cramped cubby hole with a few chairs in the center and a ring of benches along each wall. Thick curtains were drawn over the windows, casting the room into gloomy night. Despite the opulent furniture, the space reeked of cigar smoke, stale food, and spilled alcohol.

A woman was draped casually in the largest chair, one leg crossed over the other. Her black hair was threaded with silver and hung loose around her shoulders. She wore a man's shirt, unbuttoned to the navel and gaping open in a way that would have been obscene in mixed company, and her uniform slacks were so form-fitting they looked painted on. Her boots reached her knees and flared at the top like the wings of a vulture.

She looked up from examining her fingernails. She gave them the smile of a predator. "Captain Landau. We've met before, once, very briefly. I'm doubt you remember. But you made an impact." She unfolded herself from the chair and extended one hand. "Captain Isobel Ronan. At your pleasure." She winked at Fausta. "And I mean that sincerely. As much pleasure as you care to take."

Clio looked at the outstretched hand. "Sorry, did you say... *Captain?* What happened to your husband?"

Isobel waved her hand dismissively. "You said you wished to have a peaceful parlay with my ship. I'm very curious to know what business a pirate vessel has with us."

"All right." Clio took a step forward. "We'll begin with the fact that we know we're not speaking to Isobel Ronan at the moment."

"Oh?" Isobel looked down. She patted her breasts and hips as if testing to see if she was real. "I certainly seem to be myself."

Clio arched an eyebrow. "So it's just a coincidence that immediately after you encountered Granny Wise, the *Loyal Sea* transformed from a respectable privateering vessel to a brutal raiding party?"

"Ah! You know about Granny Wise. I suppose that does make a difference." She gestured at the chairs. "Please, have a seat. I think I can clear some things up."

Clio nodded for Fausta and Aravanis to sit, but she remained standing. She wouldn't sit until Isobel did.

"How much do you know about what transpired at Baleares?"

Fausta was the one who responded. "The *Loyal Sea* arrived. Isobel Ronan went missing in the forest for several days. When you returned, you claimed you'd simply gotten lost. After your ship set sail, Granny Wise was found dead in her hovel. The legends say that she hops from old, dying bodies to younger ones to achieve immortality. What we don't know is why she... or *you*... chose to leave the island instead of staying as you always have before."

Isobel laughed. "I see. There's a rather important part of the story that you also don't know. You don't know why I went to see Granny Wise in the first place." Her smile widened and she looked at each of her guests in turn. "Would anyone care to venture a guess...?"

Clio said, "Why don't you enlighten us."

"Fine." Isobel put her hands in her hair, threading it through her fingers as she turned and began pacing in a wide circle. "I went to Granny Wise because John Ronan was an absolute monster. I'm sure, if you met him, you thought he was *honorable*." She drew the word out until it was twice its length. "He was a good man. A strong captain. He cultivated that image with everyone he met. He would give you the shirt off his back and the last coin in his pocket. But the men and women of the *Loyal Sea* knew the truth. He was brutal. Cruel. He demanded perfection from everyone, most of all his wife. I was expected to present myself as his prim and proper bride at all times. Even when we were at sea."

She had reached her chair again and sat down. Clio elected to remain standing.

"If I came up short, he made sure I knew it. If he thought anyone on the crew wasn't pulling their weight, they were savagely punished. Days spent in rooms so small they couldn't move. Forbidden from eating. Given only enough water to ensure they survived. The *Loyal Sea* was a prison ship without the chains. I went to Granny Wise for a death. Poison, preferably, something that would have made him suffer horribly before he finally keeled over."

Clio crossed her arms. "Did she give you what you asked for?"

Isobel laughed. "She started talking about offering me *true* freedom, power, a lifetime of new experiences. I told her I wasn't interested, but she wouldn't listen. She kept insisting it was a better deal. I don't care how much magic you have, life in a fucking hole in the ground sounds miserable. But the power...? That intrigued me. So I agreed to it. She did her casting, and suddenly I wasn't alone in my body anymore. The old crone keeled over.

"She started moving my body around. She wanted to use my body to bury the old one in the forest. But when she started trying to move, I stopped her." Isobel raised her hand, gazed at it. She turned it over to look at the palm and chuckled lightly. "I don't think she had ever experienced that before. Someone fighting back. But I was so fucking sick of John ordering me around, controlling my every move. Suddenly I could fight back just by thinking. She was weak from the transfer, and I was so strong from holding myself back for so long. I wrapped her up in my mind. Cut off her arms and legs. Shrunk her down so she's nothing more than a voice."

Clio said, "You overthrew your husband?"

"Overthrew," Isobel said with an oddly musical tone. "Literally, darling. I threw him over the railing. It was the most effective way to mutiny I could think of. Very clean."

"And your first act was to raid a town of innocent people?"

Fausta said.

Isobel shrugged. "We required supplies. The crew deserved to be treated like kings for a change, and John didn't keep feasts aboard. So we took what we required. Once word spreads, it will serve as an example of how I'll be running the *Loyal Sea*."

Clio looked down at her hands, not surprised to see them clenched in fists. There were plenty of ships like this sailing the seas. Vicious scavengers who took what they wanted. It wasn't her place to tell them they were wrong, or avenge the victims. Yes, it helped maintain relationships with the port cities that had been targeted if she could take out their attackers. But she needed to choose her battles. At the moment, she couldn't afford to make an enemy of Isobel Ronan.

"So you have access to all of Granny Wise's memories?" Clio asked, her voice steady. "All her knowledge, her ability to perform magic? Her spells?"

Isobel nodded. "Yes."

"Then I have a favor to ask of you." She stepped forward. "Her ability to–"

Isobel held up a hand. "I apologize. You misunderstand. I don't care why you wanted to have this conversation. I don't have any interest in hearing what you have to say."

"So why allow us to board?" Clio's blood was cold now.

"As I said, John was brutal. He liked to make examples of his crew. Anyone crossed him, he could cut off a hand, a leg, your entire arm to dissuade the rest from making the same mistake. So I have a good crew of loyal men and women, but they're weak and crippled. Glass eyes. Hooks. Peg legs. It would take a month of regular meals to get them all back up to fighting weight."

She fixed her gaze on Clio.

"Of course, the three of you look to be in peak physical condition."

Fausta and Aravanis rose from their seats.

Clio advanced on Isobel. "You mean to abduct us and, what, transfer your crew to our bodies?"

Isobel nodded. "That's part of the plan, yes."

Fausta looked toward the door to the ready room. "And what exactly would the other part be?"

"Burning your ship to ashes," Isobel said calmly. "Your crew can take refuge aboard the *Loyal Sea*, or they can stay on the *Banshee* and choose between fire and drowning."

Aravanis was already at the door. She threw it open to reveal three *Loyal Sea* crewmembers in the corridor armed with a pistol, a cutlass, and a cudgel. She looked to Clio for the order to start fighting her way through them.

Clio kept her eyes locked on Isobel. "Let us pass. We're going back to our ship."

"You're more than welcome to go back," Isobel said. "But you should know, it started burning the moment you set foot into this room."

CHAPTER EIGHT

RANZI JOINED Harriet on the quarterdeck, where they watched Clio, Fausta, and Aravanis disappear into the *Loyal Sea*.

"I don't like it," Harriet said under her breath, careful not to move her lips.

"Are you looking at the crew?" Ranzi asked.

Harriet nodded slowly. "They look hungry. Desperate. Half-starved, too. All that can make a person all kinds of dangerous."

Ranzi cleared her throat. "Captain left me in command."

"That makes sense. I'm sure you've been invaluable to her these past few years."

"Can't help feeling a little out of place, given your return," Ranzi admitted. "So if you want to—"

"To disregard my wife's orders?" Harriet offered her a wry smile. "I appreciate your misgivings, Ines, but it's your place more than mine. I'll gladly follow your—"

She cut herself off, tensing as she watched a man aboard the *Loyal Sea* preparing to lob something toward the *Banshee*. Ranzi saw it as well but didn't have time to shout an order before the object was sailing through the air between them. It was a bundle of greasy rags trailing yellow flames that danced and grew stronger as it flew in a wide arc.

The rags hit their deck and exploded outward, spitting flames in every direction like a flower blooming with light. The fire settled on tarred ropes, folded canvas, the deck, and the clothes of the unfortunate souls who were standing close enough to be caught in the first blast.

"Arm yourselves!" Ranzi bellowed, racing down the stairs.

Crewmen were already trying to tamp out the flames, but it was spreading farther than they could contain. Ranzi had drawn her sword without a thought and raced to the bridge, expecting to repel a boarding party. Instead she looked across the plank to see a half dozen men surrounding the other side, guns drawn and swords at the ready, but making no move to cross over. She realized they wanted the *Banshee* crew to come to them.

Cariad was hunkered down against the gunwale, clutching Clio's scabbard to her chest. She was staring wide-eyed at the fire.

"Cut the anchors!" Ranzi shouted to her.

"What...?" Cariad snapped out of her daze and watched Ranzi hack at the first anchor holding the plank to their railing. She realized she was holding a blade and awkwardly pulled the sword from the sheath. She managed to get her hand wrapped around the hilt and moved closer so she could chop at the anchors the same way Ranzi was.

Someone aboard the *Loyal Sea* shouted and jumped onto the plank. He charged toward them, a sword raised above his head as if he meant to bring it down on them like a hammer. Cariad screamed and reacted without thinking. She stood up straighter, grabbed the hilt of Clio's sword with her other hand, and swung it in such a wide arc that Ranzi had to take a step back to avoid being sliced.

Her blade cut into the man's calf, stopping only when it hit bone. The chop was delivered with enough force that he lost balance, yelling in pain and surprise as he toppled off the side of the bridge and went flailing down to the water. Cariad stared at the blood on her blade in shock, then looked at the other men across the bridge.

"If that was an accident, don't you dare let them know," Ranzi growled under her breath.

Clio hesitated only a second longer. Then she bared her teeth at them and jabbed the sword at them in the most threatening way she could muster.

No one else risked crossing before Ranzi had cut through the anchors. Once the bridge was disconnected, the two ships began to drift apart.

"Wait, hold on, what about the captain?" Cariad asked. "The others, they're…"

"They would have done the same thing." Ranzi was too distracted by the growing fire to worry much about their missing crew. Burning ropes were cut before the fire could climb high enough to catch the sails. Buckets appeared from below decks and were spilled across the curling arms of flame that reached out to either side of the initial impact point.

Harriet's voice rose above everyone else's, telling them to stand aside. The crowd parted and she stormed forward, rolling a barrel in front of her. When she was close enough to the flames, she wedged the blade of a dagger under the barrel's lid and snapped it free.

Sand poured forth, smothering the fire as it rolled across the deck. The crew went back to knocking down the flames with whatever was at hand. Ranzi remained tense, looking for errant sparks that might threaten to grow into a second crisis, but it looked as if they had managed to keep it under control. As long as the *Loyal Sea* didn't toss any more incendiaries…

She turned to look and saw that the other ship had pulled away from the *Banshee* while they were focused on the fire.

"They're running," she said. "The *captain*…!"

"The captain is standing in front of me." Harriet grabbed Ranzi's arm hard enough to hurt, hard enough to get her attention back on the moment at hand. "Should we pursue?"

Ranzi almost tossed the question back to her. She didn't want to answer, didn't want the pressure of being the one who decided. But Clio had left her in charge, and the responsibility fell to her. She tightened her jaw and looked at her crew. Now that the fire was contained, the men who had fought it were starting to notice the injuries they'd gained while protecting their vessel. Hands and arms, legs, feet, had all been touched by flame. Faces were blackened by the smoke, and now they were started to hack and cough.

They were in no condition to pursue an enemy. Even if they caught up with the other ship, the ensuing battle would be brief and would likely not end in their favor.

"We take care of our people," Ranzi said. "We repair our vessel. We make sure that we're ready the next time we see those bastards so we can get our crew back."

Harriet's smile was restrained but unmissable. "Aye, captain," she said. "Precisely the order I would have given, in case you were curious."

"Thank you, Mrs. Landau."

She knew it was also the decision Clio would've made, which helped put her mind more at ease. But as part of the crew hurried to get their injured mates to the infirmary, and others began gauging the damage the fire had done to the deck, Ranzi went to the railing and looked at the quickly retreating *Loyal Sea* and was all too aware that three of her friends, three people who would have died for her, were aboard that ship. She had no idea what dangers they faced, or how long she had before the situation became deadly. She could only hold on to the one thing she knew for certain.

She was going to get her people back no matter the cost.

Fausta knew that any attempt to fight back against Isobel's crew would have cost them more than it earned. And even if they did somehow manage to escape the ready room alive and without grievous injury, the ship had already pulled far enough away from the *Banshee* that there was nowhere for them to go. They would have to subdue the entire crew and commandeer the vessel, and she couldn't see any way for that to happen without one or more of them getting killed.

Aravanis seemed to have come to the same conclusion, because she didn't struggle when they were put in irons. They were surrounded for the trip across the deck so she didn't have a chance to confirm if Isobel was telling the truth about the *Banshee* burning, but she could definitely smell smoke in the air. The effort of holding back her rage had her arms shaking. It took all her self-control not to lash out and grab the first throat that presented itself when the chains were removed.

She was shoved into a wooden stall with barred windows at the front and sides. Clio was put in a cage to her right, Aravanis to her left, and the doors were secured with the chains that had just been taken from their wrists.

Isobel had followed them down. She moved to stand in front of Clio's cell and wrapped her fingers around one of the bars.

"Your people went down fighting. Killed a few of my men, in fact. You should take pride in that." She smirked and rapped her middle knuckle against the bar. "Don't get too comfortable down here. We'll be back to take care of you shortly."

She turned and left, taking everyone but two men that she assigned to stand guard. Fausta was surprised Isobel had just locked them up instead of immediately switching them with three members of her crew. She'd seen for herself that she was telling the truth about their conditions. The men standing guard still had all their limbs, but their stomachs were cavernous and their skin had a deathly pallor. They were leaning against the wall, eyes half-lidded and jaws slack.

If these were the men considered fit for guard duty, she was starting to rethink the impossibility of fighting the whole crew.

"Which one you want?" The guard was still slumped against the wall, still looked moments from passing out, but his eyes swept from Aravanis, to Clio, to Fausta, and then back again. "I think I want the big one. She looks strong."

"Strong for a girl," the other guard said, and they both gave wheezing laughs.

The first one said, "Sure, I s'pose. But at least she ain't old or brown like these two."

Aravanis wrapped her hands around the bars. Fausta heard a low rumble that she quickly identified as the large Greek woman growling.

"Calm now, Penelope," Clio said, her voice fawning. "The gentleman is right. What sort of man would choose to take over any of our inferior bodies?"

The first guard snorted a laugh. "Don't be like that, sweetheart. I'm sure that body o' yours gots lots of uses."

"Sure, mayhap," Fausta said, forcing sadness into her tone. "But it's certainly not the body *I* would choose, if I was lucky enough to have a choice. A weak little thing like me..."

"Or a rickety thing like me," Clio added. "Practically at death's door myself. I pity whoever on your crew gets stuck with me. Might last longer just turning yourself in, going to prison. I'm likely to keel over where I stand."

Fausta tilted her head toward the guards. "Of course, you *do* have a choice, don't ya? I mean. Sure. Your new captain can put you into any body in the world. Young, strapping men in the prime of life. I don't know why she'd be so quick to force you into sacks like us..."

"To keep you beneath her," Aravanis said. Her voice was flat, her eyes still locked on the guards. "To be sure you won't fight back. Take this ship from her."

Clio clicked her tongue. "Ah that makes sense. She needs you just strong enough to crew the ship for her. Anything more'n that, you're liable to decide she doesn't deserve to be your captain."

One of the guards licked his lips and wrinkled his nose. "She didn't even ask us, y'know?"

"Exactly. I'll wager she takes the first young man who crosses her path for herself. And then you'll be stuck as a crew of women. Old and weak women."

"She's right," the second guard said. "We'll get to shore soon enough. Athens. Then Rome, Barcelona... We could be gods! And she wants us to settle for *this*?"

Fausta shook her head. "Offensive."

"Selfish," Clio agreed.

Aravanis just grunted.

The guard closest to the exit pushed away from the wall. "I'm going to go have a talk with some of the boys. Keep an eye on 'em."

"They ain't getting past me." The remaining guard reached down and adjusted his belt, making sure the sword hung where they could see.

Fausta turned away so he wouldn't see her smirk. They hadn't exactly solved any of their current problems, but they had laid the groundwork for dissent among the ranks. And, perhaps more importantly, they now had an idea of who they would be dealing with. Part of her felt bad about treating this crew as enemies. They were victims of John Ronan, after all, and had suffered greatly under his command. But the racism and sexism of these two men made her feel a little better about doing whatever it took to get free.

Clio had moved to the window between their cells. "Why do you think she's really waiting to make the swaps?"

Fausta looked at the guard. He had already fallen asleep standing up, chin down and lips slack, arms crossed over his chest.

"Not sure," Fausta said. "Could be the stones are vital to the process. Gotta give the soul somewhere to set before you cram it into someone else. But if they're so important, you'd think she would've taken 'em with her when she left Baleares."

"Not if Isobel was already in complete control at that point. Granny Wise might have locked that information away to keep her from getting too powerful. Whatever reason she has, we need to take advantage of it. The longer we're ourselves, the more chances we have to turn the tides."

Fausta nodded. She was confident they could get out of this situation with a little grit and determination.

She just hoped there was a ship for them to go back to when everything was said and done.

CHAPTER NINE

THE LOYAL *Sea* left the Aegean behind and sailed west for another three days. The prisoners were fed just enough to keep them alive, tasteless scraps from the mess that Clio found only barely preferable to starvation. Isobel didn't seem to be in any particular hurry to get anywhere or make any moves to follow through on her threat. The guards had even stopped showing up, leaving them alone and unbothered except when their food and water were delivered.

And so, after the initial burst of adrenaline wore off, Clio found herself more bored than anything else. Aravanis found a comfortable position in her cell and spent most hours dozing with her arms crossed over her chest. Fausta had a deck of cards in her pocket, so she and Clio killed time with all the two-person games they could think of. When they ran out of those, they invented others.

On the afternoon of the fourth day, Aravanis got to her feet and moved to the front of her cell. Clio had been in the middle of explaining why a seven of hearts and two queens meant that she had fourteen kingdoms at her command, versus Fausta's four kings, but she paused to watch the bo's'n. Aravanis never did things for no reason, and it was worth taking a moment to measure her reactions when they did happen.

"Everything all right, 'Vanis?"

"Changing course," she said.

Clio and Fausta both got to their feet. "We may have finally reached some kind of destination."

"Thank god," Fausta said. "Right now even an execution sounds nice. At least we'd be outside."

The ship continued to slow. The door swung open and Isobel strolled in, flanked by two men with rifles. Aravanis eyed the men, then looked at Clio. The captain gave a subtle shake of her head. Aravanis could take out both men easily, but the fight would be confined to an awkwardly tight space, and the men didn't have to be full-strength to get lucky with their rifles.

Isobel unlocked the cages and stepped back so the guards could secure the prisoners' wrists in chains again.

"About time you let us stretch our legs," Fausta said.

"Enjoy it," Isobel said. "This is likely going to be the last time you'll be moving around under your own power."

Clio said, "Ah, so the time is finally right. We were starting to think you were all talk."

"Unfortunately for you," Isobel said, "I just needed the right conditions."

They were escorted onto the deck and forced onto a launch. The ship was anchored alongside a small ugly rock. It had a beach, of sorts, and the rough ground was covered with patches of dead grass. The ruins of a stone watchtower stood at the highest point of the "island." It was a good place for whatever Isobel had planned; running would do them no good. There was no forest for them to take cover, and the ruins would provide no protection whatsoever.

Three men accompanied Isobel in the launch, holding guns and blades on their prisoners for the entire journey from ship to shore. Aravanis was elected to row, and Clio knew she appreciated the workout after spending so much time in a cramped room.

When they arrived on the beach, they were unloaded onto the sand where they were forced to kneel. The crewmen stood behind them, and Isobel crouched down in front of them.

"Any last words, Captain Landau?"

Clio held Isobel's gaze and said nothing.

Isobel shrugged. "Fine by me. I just thought I'd give you the opportunity." She took a pouch from her coat pocket and poured the contents onto the sand. Unlike Santiago's pouch, this one contained stones that were dull and gray. She didn't see designs on any of them and, if she was honest, she had a hard time telling the difference between them and any other stone that had already been on the beach.

"I think starting with Miss Aravanis would be the wise choice." She looked past them at her crewmen. "I'll let you decide amongst yourselves. Who wants to be the lucky first?"

Her question was met with silence. Clio sensed the men shuffling uneasily behind her. Isobel looked from one man to the next, to the next, and the smile slowly faded from her lips.

"Come now, gentlemen, no need to be shy. And don't worry about your fellow crew! There will be plenty of bodies for them in good time."

"Right," one of the crewmen said. "That's sort of the problem, Cap'n. Plenty of others out there, right? So... so w-why these ones?"

Isobel stood up. "Are you questioning me?"

"Not at all, ma'am, no." He was growing more confident. "But th-the others. We've been talking ever since you captured these'ns. And your plan to swap 'em out for us. It ain't exactly a shift any of us are excited about making."

"You're starving, weak, pathetic." She spit the last word at them. "My husband worked you to the bone. Do you remember how many of your former crewmen you tossed over the side because they were used up? I spared you from that fate. And I'm giving you a chance to start anew..."

"New?" Another crewman laughed. "This one's on death's door!"

Clio rolled her eyes. "I'm sixty-five, for Christ's sake."

"And that one is brown."

Fausta growled low in her throat but kept her eyes forward.

Isobel laughed, a sound that was like a chop of cold water in their faces. "I'm offering you a miracle, and you question the *quality?*"

"Well, it's our lives, innit?" one of the men said. "Don't we have some kind of choice?"

"You weren't given a choice at birth," Isobel snapped. "Why should this be any different?"

"It just is!"

Fausta sighed heavily. "This is all very insulting to us, you know. We're sitting right here and you're whining about how weak we are. We're tougher than any of you right now."

"You're women!" one of the men snapped.

"Very astute," Clio said. "Have you ever broken any of your fingers on purpose?"

The man behind her snorted. "I suppose you've done something that stupid, huh?"

"Me, no." Clio nodded her chin toward Aravanis. "She's pretty good at it, though."

Aravanis pulled her arm back, her hand with the newly-broken thumb slipping easily through the cuff of her chains. The man behind her grabbed her shoulder and she bent forward at the waist. She reached over her head, grabbed a handful of his hair, and pulled. He flew over her and inadvertently tackled Isobel. Aravanis got to her feet, one hand still cuffed and the chain still attached to Clio and Fausta's restraints.

The two remaining guards attacked Aravanis together. She grabbed the blade of his extended sword and cut her hand pushing it up, turning the point back toward him. He couldn't stop fast enough and the tip buried itself in his chest. Aravanis tossed him aside and threw herself at the last man standing. She didn't waste time with him; a quick uppercut to the chin sent him flying back the way he'd come. When he landed head-first on the sand, his arms and legs flexed in a momentary seizure before they relaxed and went limp.

Isobel had thrown off the man who had knocked her down and was back on her feet. She drew her dagger and rushed the prisoners. Clio saw her coming, but Fausta moved faster. She stepped between her captain and the attacker, knees bent, ready to pounce.

"We need her alive!" Clio reminded her.

Fausta made a frustrated noise and grabbed Isobel's hand when she was close enough. She twisted, disarming her, and swept the other captain's leg out from under her. Isobel stumbled and fell flat on her face, spluttering as she spit out the mouthful of sand she'd just gotten. The man Aravanis had thrown was sitting up on his knees, making no move to join in. It was just as well he didn't, because the fight was clearly finished.

Clio knelt down beside Isobel and took her weapons while the Spanish woman glared at her. There was a keyring in her pocket, which Clio also took. Isobel growled, but Clio ignored the threat in her eyes.

"You're going back to your ship with the man you still have.

You're going to leave this place. And eventually, we're going to try this meeting again. It will be a civil conversation."

She stood up and moved back from Isobel.

"Go on. Leave."

"You made an enemy today, Clio Landau." Isobel backed toward the launch. "If you survive being exiled on this rock, know that we will hunt you and your ship to the ends of the earth."

Clio exhaled sharply, unable to hide her relief. "Well, *that* is comforting. I was fairly certain you were lying about my ship's destruction, but it's nice to know for certain."

Isabel flinched and looked to make sure her crewman was preparing the launch. "Run far and fast, Clio Landau."

"Stop saying my full name, Isobel Ronan," Clio said, mimicking the woman's accent.

Isobel got into the launch and her crewman shoved off from shore. Clio unlocked her cuffs and went to free Fausta as well. As soon as they had been released, they dragged the two dead men to a spot on the beach where high tide would cover the bodies and then hopefully drag them out to sea. They stripped both men of their clothes and went through their pockets for anything worth salvaging. Fausta let out a sharp cry of victory and held up a book of matches.

Clio grinned. "See there, ladies? Nothing to worry about. Now all we have to do is wait."

Night fell.

They stayed on the beach long enough to watch the *Loyal Sea* turn and head back out to sea. Eventually its sails vanished over the horizon. As soon as it was gone, Clio was reminded of just how vast the sea really was. She didn't know exactly where they were in the Mediterranean, but it was a good bet that there was over a hundred miles of open water in every direction. Fausta went to the high ground while there was still light. She searched for any hints of ships or land, but the horizon was a hazy blue line no matter which way she turned.

They gathered dry grass and branches as kindling and built a fire in the watchtower. They used a shirt from one of the dead sailors to light it. Soon the fire was going strong, and the stone ruins acted as a chimney to channel the smoke high into the sky. Hopefully high enough that it could be seen from a great distance.

When the sun went down and the smoke wouldn't be visible,

they built a second fire outside the ruins. Clio found an outcropping and sat down, facing north. She assumed north was their best chance, but there was truly no way of knowing where a potential rescuer would come from. Or if any would pass close enough to see the light of the fire in the first place. Or, if they did see it, if they would bother to stop and investigate.

Fausta sat down next to her with a grunt, resting her arms across her knees as she looked out into the dark. "Aravanis is scouting," she said. "I told her we can see the entire island from the tower, but she insisted on doing the perimeter."

Clio smiled. "I would expect nothing less from her." Clio looked up at the expanse of stars above them. "There's a chance we've only doomed ourselves to die on this island."

Fausta shrugged. "Killing wasn't in Isobel's plan back there. What she wanted to do was worse. It was an abduction. So if we die here... well." She sighed. "I won't lie. It's very bad. We have no food, no water, and very little shelter during the day. If they don't find us in time, then at least we die as ourselves. There's comfort in that."

Clio nodded slowly. "And it's good to know the *Banshee* really is out there somewhere."

"Sh'ah!" Fausta said, half gasp and half exhale. "And it's a relief to know you weren't as certain as you acted back in the cages. I had heavy doubts."

"I had to keep hope. I smelled the smoke, as you did. Something burned. I can only hope whatever it was, they got it under control quickly and are out there looking for us." She laughed and shook her head. "I shouldn't laugh. But it would be the perfect irony for Harriet to be resurrected, even imperfectly, only to die again a week later."

"She always did live on the knife's edge." Fausta let the silence linger for several long minutes. Finally she turned to look at Clio. "How are you... coping with... that?"

Clio ran her hand through her hair, further mussing it. "I haven't a clue. On the one hand, it is her. I have no question in my mind about that. So I should feel ecstatic that she's back. But she's in such a different, unusual body, that it's not *actually* like having her back. I believe I'm not allowing myself to think anything about it yet."

"I suppose that's the best position you can take on it."

"Mm. But it's strange. Sometimes when I'm tired, or if there's a lot going on, she'll say something a-and I'll hear her voice. And I know it's probably due to working on the ship, or not eating as much as she did at Baleares, but the body is thinner and more feminine than when I've ever seen Santiago. The way she moves and stands and sits..."

"I didn't want to say anything because it sounds like I'm seeing things," Fausta said, "But even though it hasn't had time to grow, I swear her hair is getting longer."

"Yes!" Clio slapped her leg. "It's past her ears. It's only been a week. I thought maybe she was styling it differently, but there's too much."

Fausta laughed, but the sound tapered off. "It can't bode well for Santiago, can it?"

"No," Clio admitted. "And Harriet has been quite clear that she has no interest in surviving if it comes at his expense."

"I'm not certain there's much we can do about that without Granny Wise's help." She held out her hands as if weighing the good with the bad. "But on the bright side, we discovered something useful aboard the *Loyal Sea*. Granny Wise is a prisoner. We don't have to worry about making nice with a crew of pillaging bastards. We can take them out and earn a favor from the witch in the process."

Clio nodded. "That is an excellent point. It gives us an angle of attack." She looked out over the water. "Assuming we get off this rock."

"Yes. Assuming that." She brushed her hand over the ground next to her. It took a few sweeps before she got a handful of sand. She made a fist and let the sand trickle out. "We've got time, yet. I'm not even hungry."

Clio smiled. "Neither am I."

"Should I throw these back?"

Clio and Fausta turned and saw Aravanis had quietly joined them, carrying three fish speared on a long branch.

"Where in the world..." Fausta stopped herself and held up a hand, then got to her feet. "Absolutely not. Thank you, Penelope. I'll clean and cook them."

Aravanis handed over the catch, and Fausta took it to the fire. Clio also stood and clapped Aravanis on the shoulder.

"You just bought us a little extra time. Well done."

Aravanis nodded. "Hopefully it will be enough."

As she walked away, Clio turned back to look at the sea. The dark sea.

Dark, and chillingly empty.

CHAPTER TEN

WHEN CARIAD first came aboard the *Banshee*, she slept in a horrible little nook with a half dozen crew hands surrounding her. When she made her decision to join the ship permanently, Estacia had offered to share her quarters. It was a very cramped room, with just enough room for a bed and a foot locker. There was a tiny window above the bed that let in sun when they were traveling east and moonlight when they went west. It was cramped, but there was comfort in the tightness. Cariad didn't know when she had started to think of it as 'ours' rather than just Estacia's, or when she had stopped feeling like an intruder, but at the moment it was the only place on the entire ship she felt safe.

She was sitting on her side of the bed with her current journal open in her lap. Her fingers were curled around her pencil so tightly that it would leave a divot that wouldn't fade for hours. She had been chronicling their adventures faithfully, but she couldn't bring herself to put the past few days into words. A woman resurrected after nearly a decade. The ship's deck bursting into flames.

Blood on her hands.

Cariad closed the book and put down her pencil. She drew her legs up to her chest and rested her cheek on the knees. She could hear the work being done on the main deck even as they sailed west at top speed in pursuit of the *Loyal Sea*. A huge section of the deck had been cut away, burned beyond salvage, and carpenters were hard at work to replace it as quickly as possible. She couldn't help but think of it as a giant open wound, one that she felt carved into her own chest.

She didn't know how long she stayed that way before the door opened and Estacia slipped inside. The mattress sagged under her when she sat down. She reached over and massaged the base of Cariad's neck, working out the knot that had been growing there.

"Come on, love," Estacia whispered. "You have to eat. Do you want me to feed you?"

Cariad sat up. Estacia was holding a feast of one roll and a chunk of cheese. Cariad smiled despite her inner turmoil.

"I thought you were supposed to be some kind of chef," she said.

"I only cook for people I think will appreciate it." She broke off a piece of the cheese and held it up. "Here you go. Open."

Cariad took the cheese like communion. Her lips brushed Estacia's thumb and forefinger and she pursed her lips to give them a proper kiss before she pulled away.

"I killed a man," Cariad said.

"Mm-hmm." Estacia offered another piece of cheese. "We are all very grateful you did."

Cariad ignored the cheese. "Grateful..."

"He would have boarded the ship. He might have killed you or Ranzi, or who knows how many others before someone was able to do what you did. You stopped him. And you made those other bastards think twice about following him over the bridge. You defended the ship, Cariad. I know it's tearing you apart inside, because you are a good person. You even mourn the death of those who would have killed you without blinking." She offered the cheese again. "Feel the hurt. But do not let it destroy you, mm?"

Cariad considered the cheese, then accepted it onto her tongue.

"Let me show you something." She reached into her shirt pocket and withdrew something that looked like a chunk of charcoal. She handed it to Cariad.

"What is this?"

"That's a piece of the deck they're replacing right now. It's one of the planks that was completely engulfed in flames. If you had let those men across the bridge, maybe Harriet would have been distracted. Maybe they would have stabbed her in the back so she couldn't douse the flames. The fire would have spread to the lines, the sails, all across the deck. The *Banshee* would have gone to ashes. Instead, we sail. We survive to fight another day, and a killer will never draw his sword again. Don't dwell on the one life you took. Think of the many he would have taken if he continued walking this world."

Cariad took a deep breath and let it out. She took the bread and cheese from her partner and placed it on her own lap.

"Thank you, Estacia. Can I have some stew later?"

"If I think you deserve it." She leaned close and kissed Cariad's cheek. "I love you."

Cariad's heart swelled. "I love you, too."

Estacia's eyes shone. "Come to the mess later," she said softly. "I will make your stew."

"Okay."

Estacia climbed out of bed and went to the door. She gave Cariad one more glance, then slipped out of the room.

Cariad grinned and tore off a piece of the bread. She chewed it slowly, then put aside the food and opened her book again.

I said the words, she wrote. *I heard them. And I said them in reply. And I finally, finally, finally meant them.*

Harriet Landau stood on the quarterdeck and watched the carpenters at work. The deck was starting to look whole again, which meant soon the crew would be able to focus a hundred percent on the search for the *Loyal Sea*. Tis Common was in the crow's nest for nearly sixteen hours a day, the most Harriet felt comfortable having a single person at the station. Most people risked going blind spending so much time staring out at the sun reflecting off the water, but Common had a pair of shaded glass lenses she could affix over her eyes that helped block most of the light.

Ranzi came up to join Harriet at the helm. She had been supervising the work, and gave a nod of approval as she approached. Though Ranzi had been left in command, the changing circumstances of Clio's abduction led Harriet to have a change of heart. Ranzi felt more comfortable in a support position, while captaining came naturally to Harriet after a lifetime of it. A day after they lost sight of the *Loyal Sea*, Harriet accepted Clio's cutlass and resumed command of the *Banshee*.

"They're moving as quick as they can without cutting corners or running themselves to exhaustion. We're lucky we had enough lumber to cover the gap, but we'll be wanting to pick up more to refresh. Just in case there are other incidents." She looked back down at the workers. "We should be back to full strength by tomorrow morning."

"Good," Harriet said, nodding. "I look forward to presenting Clio with a fully-intact ship when we get her back."

Ranzi started to say something, then pressed her lips together.

"You have thoughts on that?"

"Concerns," Ranzi said. "We don't know why things went so sideways, so fast. All we know is they tried torching our ship and then scarpered off with three of our people aboard. Basically, we stopped to have a chat and they responded by poking us in the eye and shooting us in the foot. I'm not sure we can guarantee they'll be... intact, healthy, and unharmed even if we are able to catch up to them."

Harriet took a deep breath and let it out before she turned to face Ranzi. "We'll not worry about that until we are presented with more facts. At the moment, they exist as we last saw them. If we start worrying about what *may* have happened in the interim, we will find reasons to give up on them. I won't be party to that. Understood?"

"Yes, ma'am." Ranzi started to leave, then turned back. "May I say one more thing...?"

"You may."

Ranzi came closer and lowered her voice so there was no chance of being overheard. "We have every reason to believe Granny Wise was aboard that ship. We know that the people aboard that ship are acting with reckless cruelty and disregard for the lives of others. With that information, there is a chance that when Clio, Fausta, and Aravanis return to us, they won't be themselves anymore. We may be allowed to rescue them as a ploy to install spies aboard the *Banshee*."

"A Trojan horse," Harriet said.

"Mm," Ranzi said in agreement.

"Your concern has been noted." Ranzi started to leave, but Harriet called her back. "Ines. I have never, and *would* never abide sycophants and weasels who blindly agree with whatever their captain says. You hesitated to contradict me when I said we'd get Clio back. I don't mind the contradiction, but I am irritated by the fact you almost didn't do it."

Ranzi said, "I wouldn't have hesitated if it was normal ship's business. This is your wife."

Harriet nodded. "I see."

"But your speech was good. I've taken it to heart."

Harriet laughed. "Good."

Ranzi winked and headed back down to the main deck. Harriet gripped the wheel and faced ahead again, scanning the horizon for sails.

Occasionally she caught a glimpse of her hands and was caught short by the sight. She extended her fingers and furrowed her brow. They were long and thin, like hers, but the fingernails looked odd. She'd never particularly noticed her own fingernails, but these were so alien that she was unsettled by the sight of them at the end of her hand.

Everything about this body was alien to her. Santiago was taller than her, wider than her, his arms and legs longer. His ears itched. She couldn't remember her ears ever itching. She wondered if it was some kind of bug. Lice or fleas or something. But he seemed relatively clean elsewhere. It was just her damn ears that wouldn't leave her alone.

She refused to think about how small his bladder was. She tried to black out any instances when action was required. The only good thing about that ordeal was how quick she could be finished with it.

Santiago was much quieter the past few days. At first she put it up to her heightened emotions. She was so focused on Clio and what might be happening to her on the *Loyal Sea* that he wasn't being given a chance to speak up. But moments like this, when there was just smooth sailing, strong winds, and open ocean all around, she expected to hear some rumbling of his thoughts at the back of her mind. But there was nothing.

She had noticed other changes as well. When she first "woke up," Santiago's hair had been a bit shaggy but manageable. Now, barely a week later, she had to tie it back to keep it out of her face. It shouldn't have been growing so quickly. Even accounting for the variations of one body versus another, that wasn't natural. The body had also lost weight. The hips seemed more shapely.

She felt less like an intruder with every passing day, and she was terrified of what it might indicate.

Just give me long enough to find Clio, she thought. *Let me find her, save her, know she's okay. I'll give your body back to you even if it means surrendering to my fate. I just can't leave her in peril.*

Harriet remembered a young woman standing on a cliff, near a field of daisies. The woman was laughing, and when she smiled the sky seemed to dim around her because she was so much more beautiful than the sun. She swept her hair out of her face with both hands and then danced to a song only she could hear. Harriet saw her hand - Santiago's hand - reach out to the woman. Just before he reached her, she vanished in a burst of smoke and sand.

If I die in pursuit of lost love, I will consider it a noble sacrifice.

Harriet couldn't have said if it was her thought or Santiago's, but she was willing to accept there was enough of a gray area that she could consider it an agreement.

They sailed for hours with no clear destination. Ever westward, with Harriet's mind busy trying to figure out where Captain Ronan would drop anchor next. It was a futile exercise that mainly just succeeded in reminding her of how long she'd been gone. Any information she had about the port towns she'd once known like the back of her hand would be eight years out of date. That was a lifetime in places like this, sometimes literally. She would be more lost than the greenest sailor on the boat, and that was a very difficult fact to accept.

When the sun was close enough to touch the horizon, Harriet decided she had spent enough time at the helm. She needed to rest her eyes, her mind, and Santiago's body in equal measure. She'd barely eaten anything in the days since Clio went missing, which could have accounted for some of the weight loss she'd noticed. She would hand the ship over to Ranzi and then-

"*Smoke!*"

The exhaustion fled from Harriet at the shout. Her eyes snapped to the horizon, scanning it for what Common might have seen from her perch.

There. A definite column of smoke, just a few degrees south of their current heading. She tightened her grip on the handles of the wheel to adjust course.

It might not be Clio, but it might have been another victim that ran afoul of the *Loyal Sea*. Even if it was just a random disaster, she couldn't bring herself to sail past without checking to see if they could render assistance. It's what she would hope someone would do for her crew if their situations were reversed.

They approached the source of the smoke with agonizing

slowness. By the time the sun crossed the horizon line and darkened the sky, they were close enough to see the flames creating the distress signal. It was burning in a watchtower on what looked like an incredibly tiny rock. Shadows passing in front of the fire proved there was at least one person walking around on the island, and Harriet forced herself to keep calm. She wouldn't allow herself to hope, not this early.

Ranzi began preparing the launch, preparing to head out with Delfina and a package of food and canteens of water. Harriet ordered the signal gun to be fired to announce their presence. There was movement on the shore in response; one person with arms waving stepped forward to be silhouetted by the fire.

"Please, please," Harriet muttered.

There was nothing she could do but wait, as agonizing as that thought was. She handed the helm over to a crewman and went down to the deck. Cariad, the journalist, was at the railing focused on the fire. She was squinting, which indicated she was trying to spot more bodies on the island. She jumped when Harriet joined her.

"I'm sure it will be good news."

"Even if it's not," Harriet said, "it's someone in need. I won't regret the time spent coming here."

Cariad said, "Are you trying to convince me or yourself?"

"Are you asking so you'll be sure to get it right in your book?"

Cariad turned away. Harriet was on the verge of apologizing when the writer spoke again. "Clio still has the book I wrote. The one about everyone. It's the only copy. You're more than welcome to read it yourself if you'd like to put your mind at ease."

"That won't be necessary. You have Clio's trust. That's enough for you to have mine."

Cariad looked at her again. "I tried very hard to be honest about everyone I wrote about. I used their own words. I... respect these women." She smiled and looked around the deck. "They're amazing. I just want people to know about them even if the worst happens. Like... like you. When you were hanged. You only lived in their memories. And if Clio is gone..." She crossed herself, a reflexive motion. "The memory of you would have gone with her. I don't want that to happen."

Harriet made a quiet sound of contemplation. "I can appreciate that. Maybe even respect it."

Someone on the island fired a gun in the air. Once, twice,

thrice. Harriet's heart leapt, and she finally allowed herself to hope.

"Three shots," Cariad said. "Does that mean three people...?"

"That's how I'm choosing to interpret the message, yes." She clapped Cariad on the shoulder. "Go down to the mess and tell your girl to prepare a proper meal. Even if it isn't our girls, they're bound to be hungry when they get here."

Cariad nodded and disappeared across the deck.

Harriet looked at the island and watched the launch, waiting for the people in the dark to climb aboard and start back to the ship.

"I know you used up a miracle to get me back, Clio," Harriet said under her breath. "Please, please tell me you kept one for yourself..."

CHAPTER ELEVEN

CLIO QUICKLY discovered it was easier to sleep than anything else. It conserved energy, it kept her from thinking about how thirsty she was, and it prevented her from obsessively scanning the horizon for sails. It would only have been counterproductive to keep looking. Eventually mirages would begin forming, at best, and at worst, constantly staring at an unchanging sun and sky and sea would have blinded her. So she went up to the watchtower, found a spot in the shade, and rested against the crumbling stone with her eyes closed.

Night had fallen again. It had been a whole night and day on the island. Her mouth was so dry that she could hear the bones of her jaw clicking. They had boiled some seawater, but it tasted vile, so they only drank the bare minimum to prevent dehydration. The fish had been great the first night, but they'd only eaten enough to take the edge off. And it was a good thing they saved the rest, because Aravanis was yet to catch more. They'd all tried, but her attempt was their only success so far.

The night was going to be endless. And then there would be another endless day. And if they weren't found by the time the sun set again... Well, she didn't have to worry about getting through another night. If they weren't found by then, it would be over.

In her sleep, she heard thunder. Loud cracks, followed by shouting. It wasn't worth opening her eyes to watch the weather. Weather would put out their fire, would obscure the smoke signals. Weather would doom them even faster. She didn't want to see the rains that would destroy their chances of rescue.

"Clio..."

She turned her head toward the memory of Delfina's voice. Sweet and soft. She smiled. "Hi."

"Hello. Can you drink this for me, darling?"

"Boil it."

Her words were slurred, but Delfina still understood. "No, love, this is good water. Here you go. Tilt your head back for me."

Something touched Clio's lips. She opened her mouth and delicious, cold, fresh water poured onto her tongue. It woke her up, and she angled her neck forward to get closer.

"Careful, careful," Delfina said. "It's all right. Take your time."

There were three sharp cracks. Gunshots, Clio realized, not thunder. She opened her eyes and saw Delfina, an actual living human, kneeling next to her. Beyond her, Ranzi was standing next to the launch, holstering her weapon while Fausta and Aravanis drained canteens of their own. Clio furrowed her brow at them, then looked at Delfina.

"We're rescued?"

"It looks that way, Captain." She cupped Clio's cheek. "We'll give you a second to rest, and then I'll help you onto the launch."

Clio was up on her feet with one arm draped across Delfina's shoulders before she realized she was actually awake. She lifted her head and looked at the launch again.

"Izzit a rescue...?" she slurred.

"Yes, love. You're rescued."

"Fausta...? And 'Vanis...?"

"They're fine."

"The ship..."

"Damaged, but it's been repaired. Everything and everyone is secure, Captain."

Clio sighed. "Okay, good."

With that, she surrendered her grip on consciousness and let herself slump heavily against the doctor's side.

The next thing she saw was the support beams above her bed in the infirmary. She blinked them into focus and then rolled her head across the pillow to see whose weight was pressing down the mattress. Harriet was backlit by a lantern. Her hair was long enough to be tied back, and the shape of her body was so familiar, that for a moment she allowed herself to believe they'd somehow managed to truly bring her back to life.

But the belief only lasted for a moment. She made a quiet sound of pain as she shifted, and Harriet looked at her.

"Clio...? Love, are you...?"

"I think I'm here," she groaned. "The others?"

"Aravanis and Fausta are recovering nicely. Fausta implied you barely ate. Saved the rations for them."

"Fish weren't a guarantee." Clio's head was pounding. "Captain Ronan is dead. His~"

Harriet was already nodding. "Fausta told us the whole story. Isobel Ronan. Ranzi is asking around to see if anyone onboard has had any dealings with her. She sounds like a real piece of work."

"That's putting it mildly. But at least it solves one of our problems..."

"Yes, Fausta explained that as well." Harriet looked down at her hands. "I'm sure you've noticed there have been a few changes in the days you were gone."

Clio said, "It's becoming harder to ignore. Your voice is even different."

"What?"

"Santiago is a Spaniard. You're speaking like you just boarded the ship from London."

Harriet put a hand to her throat. "I hadn't even noticed."

Clio carefully pushed herself up in the bed. "We may have to accept that we don't have a choice in what happens to Santiago."

"We have a choice. Of course we do."

"Even if I'm willing to entertain the possibility of letting you go again, how would that happen? Do you know a way you can... can... leave? You said it was like he was in another room of the same house. Is there a door you can open? A window to crawl through?"

Harriet didn't answer.

"These changes are happening to you so quickly. Even if we found the *Loyal Sea* tomorrow, Granny Wise is as much a prisoner as Santiago is. We can't kill Isobel Ronan, we can't force the witch out of her, I'm fairly certain we can't convince her to help us... We're quickly passing the point of no return. And I'm sorry, but I won't pretend to be distraught over that. Santiago is a great man, and it's terrible to think of him being lost this way, but... if it means having you back, I won't call that a tragedy."

"He seems to get quieter every hour," Harriet said. "At first I thought he just didn't have anything to say, but the longer this goes on, I think... maybe he can't."

Clio said, "You can feel him, though? And you know his thoughts, his feelings?"

Harriet nodded. "I'm very aware of him."

"Okay," Clio said carefully. "I think we can assume it goes both ways. He knows how you feel about taking over his body. He knows you're doing everything in your power to make it right. He'll know that you tried to do right by him."

"I hope so." Harriet reached out and took Clio's hand. She squeezed it, still not looking her in the eye. "I never let myself believe you were gone. Even though you were on that ship, with that horrible crew. I couldn't entertain the idea you wouldn't come back. And I still couldn't sleep. I couldn't eat. I couldn't stop until I knew for certain you were safe. I can't imagine how you survived for eight years."

"In a way I was lucky," Clio said. "I knew you wouldn't be coming back. I saw your..." She bit off the last word. "It was easier, though so much more painful. Without the false hope. Without lying to myself. But the grief lasted so much longer. And it was so deep. Fausta and Ranzi kept us afloat for months while I was utterly useless in my cabin."

Harriet managed a smile. "It's good to know I was missed."

"I didn't know who I was without you. It was like losing my memory all over again."

"But you found yourself."

Clio nodded. "Eventually. And with help." She picked up Harriet's hand, brought it to her lips. She kissed the knuckles, then pressed them to her cheek. "Can you help me to my cabin? Our cabin. Am I allowed to rest there, or does Delfina have me confined here?"

"I think she'd understand needing your own bed."

Harriet slipped off the mattress. She turned and helped Clio stand. She ducked under Clio's right arm, then slipped her arm around Clio's waist.

"Ready?"

"Go slowly."

Harriet nodded.

They left the infirmary and slowly headed up through the ship, stopped by every crew member they passed so they could welcome Clio back to the ship. Estacia gave her a very careful, very restrained hug and a kiss on the cheek and assured her that as soon as she was up to having a full meal, her favorite feast would be on the menu. Tis Common even climbed down from the lookout perch when she realized Clio was up and around, welcoming her back to the ship.

When they finally reached her cabin, Harriet closed the door. Clio was able to get to the desk on her own to light a lantern. It barely did anything to push back the shadows, but it was enough to see by. Harriet pressed her back to the door.

"You're beloved."

"They liked me before I became captain," Clio said, lowering herself carefully onto the bed. "I was just coasting off your goodwill, and they're used to me now."

Harriet shook her head. "No, I saw them when you were lost. This is loyalty." She knelt in front of Clio and rested her hands on her thighs. "They love you. They respect you. You are their leader, Clio, and I wouldn't want anyone else commanding my ship. I knew you would be a great captain. I'm so lucky I get to see for certain before... anything else happens."

Clio smiled sadly. She touched Harriet's cheek. "We used to sit like this every night. You would take off my boots at the end of a long day." She wiggled her toes; she'd woken barefoot in the infirmary, her boots and belt removed by Delfina, she assumed.

Harriet nodded. "And then I would kiss you. And then I would help you undress. And..." Her eyes dropped to Clio's lap. She pulled her hands back to Clio's knees.

Clio put her hands on top of Harriet's to keep them there. "I've missed you so much, Harriet."

She leaned forward, hesitating only a second before closing the distance. Harriet's lips were stiff when they first touched, but they softened and then parted for her. Harriet moaned softly and moved her hands higher again. Her fingers tightened as if she was holding tight to keep herself from falling. Clio kept the kiss as chaste as possible, holding it for as long as she dared before pulling back.

"I know it's not the same as you," Harriet said quietly. "To me, it feels like just a few days ago when everything was normal. But to be here, with you, but... apart. Not able to kiss you. Or touch you." She flinched as if admitting that caused her physical pain. "It's been torture, my love."

Clio stared into Harriet's eyes. After a few seconds, she looked around the bed. Finding nothing, she pointed to the footlocker.

"Get me a stocking. Just one."

Harriet furrowed her brow but shifted position to reach the plywood crate at the end of the bed. She had to dig a bit before she found a white knee-length stocking. She moved back to where she'd been kneeling and handed it to Clio. Clio threaded it between her fingers and pulled it straight, then brought it up and pressed the cotton against her eyes. She bowed her head and pulled the ends of the stocking around to tie a knot at the base of her skull.

"What are you doing?" Harriet asked, a laugh in her voice.

Clio reached for her again, finding her cheeks and gently stroking them. Harriet turned her head to brush her cheek against Clio's palm.

"You are Harriet Landau. You have thick eyebrows that should make you look angry all the time, but your eyes soften them just enough. Your blue eyes. The bluest I've ever seen, with little flecks of green if the water is right." She reached back to untie Harriet's ponytail, running her fingers through it. "Your hair... is long. Center-parted. It was solid black when we met, but the last time I saw you, it was the color of ash and steel."

"Clio..."

"Shh." Clio brushed her thumb across Harriet's lips. "I feel you. I hear your voice when you speak. And now, love, I see you again, as lovely as the last time we were in this room together."

Harriet parted her lips and grazed the pad of Clio's thumb with her teeth. Clio sucked in a breath.

Then they were kissing again, Harriet rising up, pushing Clio down onto the mattress without breaking apart. Harriet laid on top of her, between her legs, and reached for the tie of her pants. Clio moaned and turned her head, and Harriet began kissing along Clio's cheek, down to her throat. Harriet's left hand got her pants open and then reached inside.

"Are you sure this is okay?" Clio gasped and lifted her hips to meet Harriet.

Harriet sat up, inadvertently pressing herself against the crotch of Clio's trousers. "Is it okay with you...? Considering I'm... my..."

"I am intrigued by that." Clio's voice shuddered. "It's you. It's... d-different. But it's still you. I mean that it's Santiago's body. If he would be unwilling to~"

"I think he's willing," Harriet said.

"How can you be sure?"

"Because I'm not controlling my left arm," she admitted.

"Oh." Clio shivered underneath her. "I would prefer it if you only touch me with your *right* arm then. At least until you're back in control."

Harriet's left arm went limp so suddenly that she couldn't help but laugh. She lifted it, flexed her fingers, and then touched Clio's lips.

"I think Santiago is also turning a blind eye to what's about to happen."

Clio laughed and clung to Harriet's neck while Harriet undid Clio's pants and pushed them down, their bodies twisting so she could kick them off and get them out of the way. Clio felt something against her hip, ignoring it as best she could. She just knew it was part of Harriet, a new part, a different part. Harriet stroked the inside of Clio's thigh and then touched her with two fingers.

"God I've missed you," Clio gasped.

"I've been aching to do this," Harriet whispered.

"Please."

Harriet shifted her weight and reached a hand between them. Clio held her breath. There was a moment of awkward fumbling, when sensitive flesh rubbed sensitive folds and they both gasped in painful pleasure. Harriet went very still and then laughed quietly and whispered, "Okay. It's okay. It was almost... over, I think..."

Clio laughed and ran her hands over Clio's face. She tried not to venture down to her chest, or to her arms. She didn't want to spoil the illusion. At the moment, with her eyes covered, even the heavy breathing and gasps above her sounded like Harriet. Even the fingers moving against her felt like a familiar caress she'd long ago given up on feeling again.

"Harriet," she whispered.

"I'm here, my love," Harriet whispered.

And then Harriet was inside her.

They both cried out, but Clio was louder. She wrapped her legs around Harriet's waist, hooked her ankles together, and pulled her forward. Harriet grunted and groaned, one step away from thrashing on top of her. Clio grabbed a handful of Harriet's hair and pulled her head down, getting her lips up close.

"Take your time, love."

"I can't," Harriet groaned. "I'm... fuck, Clio..."

"Shh, slow slow slow," Clio chanted, saying the words in the rhythm she wanted Harriet to take. "Slow, my love, slow, Harriet... that's it, darling..."

Harriet matched Clio's words until they were moving together, following the sway of the ship. Harriet whimpered again and pressed her cheek against Clio's shoulder.

Suddenly she went stiff, pulled back quickly, and reached between their bodies. Clio went still, imagining what was happening from the way the mattress shook under Harriet's movements. She was twitching, spasms racking her body, and then she groaned and cried out with release. Clio didn't feel anything on her skin, so she assumed Harriet had finished in her own hand.

"Wasn't expecting that..." Harriet said breathlessly.

Clio chuckled. "It was certainly different."

Harriet stretched for something to wipe her hand off with. Clio idly put a hand between her legs and started rubbing, intending to finish herself off.

Harriet said, "No, stop that... I may be finished but I'm not done."

"Oh really."

"Really."

Harriet settled between Clio's legs and kissed her thighs, stomach, hips. Clio put her hands in Harriet's hair and knew who was in bed with her. There was no doubt, no question, no confusion. When she felt lips and a tongue on her, goosebumps spread out across her whole body because it was the touch she'd ached for since losing Harriet. The others she'd been with had been passable, had scratched the itch, gotten her through lonely nights, but this...

This was her wife.

"You're my wife," Clio gasped.

Harriet pressed her tongue against Clio's sex, curled the tip, and hummed. Clio arched her back off the bed and tightened her grip on Harriet's hair.

"*Harriet...*" She bit off the name and hissed through her teeth as she came. She breathed in deeply and then, as she exhaled it all, she whispered, "I love you, I love you, I love you, I love you."

When she was aware enough to think again, she plucked at the stocking in an attempt to yank it off. Harriet whispered, "Let me, let me," and gently lifted her head. She worked the knot blindly and then chuckled as she dug her fingernails into it. "God, how did tight did you make this?"

"I'm a sailor," Clio laughed, enjoying the way Harriet's body was pressing against hers. "Here, just pull it up..."

She slipped the stocking over her head and Harriet tossed it aside. Then she cupped Clio's face and kissed her.

"That's the first time you've said you loved me since I came back," she said when the kiss ended. "You've *called* me love... but this is the first time you actually said it."

Clio brushed the backs of her fingers down the front of Harriet's chest. "It's the first time I didn't have to look past your... situation..." She moved her hand up and touched the bridge of Harriet's nose, then her lips, her chin, and jaw.

"I see you," she said. "And I love you, Harriet. I love you so very much."

A tear dropped from Harriet's cheek, landing on Clio's collarbone. "And I love you, Clio."

Harriet lowered herself, covering Clio's body completely as they kissed again. In the darkness, with the changes the body had already gone through, it was all but impossible to see any differences between the person pinning her down and the woman she'd sworn her heart to. She swore to herself she would also stop looking for those differences in the bright light of day and focus on what she knew to be true with all her heart.

Her wife was back.

CHAPTER THIRTEEN

THE BANSHEE sailed on. Clio, Fausta, and Aravanis quickly recovered from their ordeal on the island, and Delfina cleared them all for full duty after a few days of taking it easy. The ship went from port to port in search of word about the *Loyal Sea*'s next destination, but it seemed as if Isobel Ronan was keeping her head down for the time being. After hearing Fausta's account of everything that had happened aboard the other ship, along with how they ended up left behind, Cariad assumed she might also be dealing with a mutiny from her remaining crew.

Cariad spent the long days of sailing in her quarters with Granny Wise's journal. Ranzi had taken it from the old witch's hovel but the handwriting was so atrocious that it might as well have been in code. Cariad managed to find enough actual words that she knew it was in English, so she was filling the hours trying to 'translate' as much of it as possible.

The fourth morning after their rescue of Captain Landau, Cariad ran across the deck with Granny Wise's book in one hand and a pen in the other. She nearly collided with Ranzi and, in lieu of an apology, demanded to know where the captain was.

"In her quarters. But~"

Cariad was already out of earshot. She headed below deck and pounded hard on Clio's door. She heard a noise from within and took it as invitation to enter.

"Captain, I found a... oh."

She quickly turned her back, but the sight had been burned onto the back of her eyelids. Clio and Harriet, on the edge of the bed, both clothed but with the catches and buttons completely undone. The captain's hand wrapped around... and Harriet's head bowed to the captain's chest...

Cariad's cheeks burned. "Apologies, but it *is* an urgent matter..."

"One would hope," Clio said over the sound of rustling clothes. "You can stop averting you eyes, Miss Baillie."

Cariad looked out the corner of her eye first, then turned back around. Harriet's shirt was still unbuttoned, baring her chest. It seemed obscene, but Cariad knew that was ridiculous. It was a man's chest, and plenty of the other men on the ship went around bare-chested. But Harriet was... *Harriet*. She was treated as a woman, referred to as such, and Cariad found the exposure indecent. She pressed her lips together and decided to ignore it for the time being. What she had to say was far more important.

"I've figured out part of the book," Cariad said. "The journal of Granny Wise. I've been trying to make sense of the chicken scratch ever since Ranzi brought it back, and I think I've found something interesting. You said that Isobel didn't even attempt to transfer her crew into your bodies until you were at the island, correct?"

Clio nodded. "That's right."

"There's a reason. The transfer has to happen on dry land. It has something to do with a connection to the earth, the sacred ground, the source of all."

"But we were on the ship when Harriet went into Santiago's body," Clio said. "Nowhere near dry land. How did that happen?"

"Not a clue." She held up the book and gestured at the cover. "I haven't even started on the long and complicated paragraphs about *why*. Maybe it's just easier on land, or more focused. Harriet didn't choose to possess Santiago. Maybe being on land helps direct where the soul goes. But that's all just speculation. I figured decoding the *how* was more important at the moment."

"I concur," Clio said. "If Isobel believed the ritual needed to happen on dry land, we should assume that's the optimal situation for it."

"So." Cariad nodded as if her point had been made.

Clio raised her eyebrows. "Yes?"

"So I did," Cariad explained. "I found the how."

Harriet stood up. "You know how to reverse the spell?"

Cariad nodded. "I think so. I'm fairly certain." She opened the book and flipped through the pages. "Once I got a feel for her handwriting, it started to come a bit easier. The shape of her letters isn't always uniform, but there's a range for the vowels that my eyes started picking out..."

Harriet said, "I think I finally see why you kept this girly around, Clio."

"Thank you, Missus Landau." She beamed proudly.

Clio crossed her arms over her chest. "Very well, Miss Baillie. What about the other hurdle?"

Cariad's smile faded. "The other...?"

"You can remove Harriet from Santiago's body? Fantastic." She held her hands out palm-up. "Where does it go? We don't have a body waiting, unless you know of someone lying braindead in the crew's quarters."

Harriet's voice was low and flat, as if she was accepting defeat. "She can just put me back into the stone." She looked at Cariad. "Right? You can put me into one of those stones as easily as into a new body."

Clio jabbed a finger at Cariad before she could open her mouth to reply. "Don't answer that. It is not an option."

"Clio, love, we agreed~"

"I know what we agreed," Clio said. "But I know you understand what you're asking me to do. And I know you understand how impossible it is. I finally have you back. I won't put you into a fucking rock and hope that someday you'll come back again."

Harriet lowered her head. "Clio... this is not fair to Santiago. Look what I've already done to his body. There may be a point of no return where he won't recover."

"Are you so sure we haven't already crossed that line?" Clio asked.

Harriet sighed heavily. "I won't live at someone else's expense."

"That's exactly what you asked of us," Clio snapped. "You sacrificed yourself all those years ago so Ranzi and Aravanis could get to safety. Would it be so bad? A life for a life..."

"Stop," Harriet said. "Santiago has been extremely

accommodating of this entire situation, but I don't know how intentional that is. He may decide he's had enough. He may take offense that you're treating him so expendably and retake the body. Look what happened to Granny Wise with Isobel Ronan. The host can stay in command, apparently. And then I'll be lost anyway. I have to surrender his body. It's the proper thing to do. It's the only moral thing to do."

Cariad cleared her throat.

"Why are you still here?" Clio snapped.

"Well," Cariad said, "I-I think... I think Harriet is correct~"

"No one asked you, Miss Baillie."

Cariad held up her hands. "Noted, Captain. But there is an option besides the stone which I think you would be amenable to."

They both looked at her expectantly. Cariad inadvertently shrank under their attention.

"I-it's just that Captain, you can't give Harriet up again. Understandably, no one should be asked to make such a sacrifice. A-and, and, Missus Landau, you refuse to remain in the body of an unwilling host who is being physically changed without his consent. It seems, um, well. We could ask someone to, to, to, uh... take over."

Harriet said, "Take over what?"

"Being host to you. Your, your soul. Or whatever this actually is. It could be their, um, informed decision. You're only... in... Santiago because of happenstance. You could choose a more appropriate body to take over. Less chance of, um, ch-ch-changes. Physically speaking."

They were both quiet. Harriet watched Clio closely, but the captain didn't betray any emotions.

"Who would ever agree to such a thing?" Harriet said.

Cariad shrugged. "I suppose we won't know until we ask. There could be any number of reasons someone might agree. I never would, so I can't think of any justifications. But someone out there... we have no idea what they might be going through. The idea of handing the reins over to someone else might be very appealing."

Silence filled the room like a held breath until Clio broke it. "I suppose there's no harm in asking." She looked at Cariad. "And if someone *does* agree, you're confident you can make it happen? Pull Harriet from one body and place her in another of our choosing?"

"Oh! Oh yes." She opened the book and flipped through a few pages. Then she nodded. "Yes, I'm fairly certain. And I have until we reach land to be completely sure."

Clio chewed on her bottom lip.

"I'm willing," Harriet said.

Clio finally nodded. "Then I am as well."

Harriet gestured at the door. "In that case, I see no reason to delay."

"Right."

Clio stepped between Harriet and Cariad, opened the door, and walked with purpose out of her cabin. Harriet followed and Cariad closed the door behind her as she hurried to catch up.

Clio went directly to the quarterdeck. Fausta was at the helm, and Aravanis saw the captain's approach and moved to intercept her. When Clio took her position at the rail, Aravanis was at her side with the bo's'n whistle at the ready to summon the crew. Cariad and Harriet stood a few steps away, also watching. Clio stared down at the crew, some of whom had noticed her but hadn't stopped going about their business.

When thirty seconds passed, Aravanis turned her head slightly to appraise Clio's profile. When another thirty seconds passed, Aravanis lifted the whistle slightly.

"Ma'am...?"

Clio shook her head. She turned away from the rail and went to Harriet.

"I can't," Clio said. "I'm essentially asking them to commit suicide for me. I can't do that."

Harriet said, "If it's their choice—"

"No," Clio snapped. She ran her hand through her hair, creating a new arrangement of the spikes and tangles. When she raised her head, she was looking at Cariad. "You said you were 'fairly certain' you can reverse the swap, right? I need a confident guarantee."

"Well," Cariad said, "at the moment I don't think I can give you complete assurance. But! But. If we do the procedure and Harriet successfully leaves Santiago's body to someone else, then I will have confirmed I've correctly deciphered the spell. If I got it wrong, she'll just stay where she is. So... so if the swap happens, I am certain I can do it again. Yes."

Clio nodded. "That's good enough for me. I volunteer."

Cariad, Harriet, and Fausta all said, "What?" at the same time, at different levels of panic. Harriet's voice was the highest, drowning out the others. She stepped forward, eyes flashing with anger.

"You can't, Clio."

"I'm the only one who can. You're my wife. I can't ask anyone else to give up~"

Fausta said, "As the captain of this ship, you cannot be compromised by~"

"I won't be compromised, Fausta, I'm~"

"If I start taking over..." Harriet shook her head.

Clio held her hands up to stop everyone's chattering. "We've seen both possibilities with a shared consciousness. Harriet completely overwhelmed Santiago. But Isobel managed to silence Granny Wise, someone I assume has far more experience with this sort of thing than Isobel does. So it's possible there's a happy medium where Harriet and I can coexist peacefully. At least while we're seeking a more permanent solution."

"And if we can't?" Harriet asked. "If it becomes necessary to put me back in the stone?"

"Then..." Clio held her hands out to either side. "Then that's what we'll do. You have my word. And if I'm lying, then you'll know when we do the swap."

Harriet said, "At which point it will be too late."

Clio shrugged. "So you'll just have to trust me. Like always."

Harriet pressed her lips together and looked down at her feet. They were still bare, since she hadn't taken the time to fully dress when she left Clio's cabin.

"The fact remains that we *must* get Santiago's body back to him. You may be right that this is the best option. So if you are willing, then... then... yes. I agree as well."

Clio sighed with relief and turned to Fausta. "Take us to the first island you see. The ritual has to happen on dry land."

Fausta nodded, eyeing the other women skeptically. "You're all sure about this?"

"We're sure that it's the best option," Harriet said. "And that we have a distinct lack of other options at this point. I can either agree with Clio's plan or risk killing Santiago. I would rather try."

"Fair," Fausta said. "I'll aim us toward the first piece of green we see."

Clio nodded her thanks and patted Fausta on the shoulder as she left the quarterdeck.

Harriet moved closer to Cariad and nodded at the book. "I know you had to have a lot of faith in yourself to even suggest this plan."

"I do," Cariad said.

"I trust that. I do. But perhaps you could spend the time until we find an island..."

Cariad knocked her knuckles against the book and nodded. "Research and study," she said. "Without question. Absolutely, I will."

"Good girl."

Harriet headed down to the deck as well, crossing toward the bow instead of returning to Clio's cabin. Cariad saw that Fausta had also noticed that the two Landau women had chosen to separate from each other. Fausta didn't say anything, so Cariad decided she wouldn't be the one to break the silence. She clutched the journal to her chest and went to find somewhere quiet she could focus.

The lives of Harriet Landau and Santiago Zeno were in her hands. There were still things she needed in order to make sure everything went the way they hoped.

First and foremost, she needed to get her hands on a gun.

It only took a few hours for Tis Common to spot an appropriate island. Clio went to the helm to watch as they approached. It was a little larger than the rock Isobel had stranded them on. It was essentially a long flat beach with handful of rocky outcroppings. The only thing that mattered to Clio was that it was large enough for them to take the launch ashore, and it seemed to have plenty of room for the ritual.

The sun was steadily rolling toward the horizon. Clio looked over at Cariad, who had been asked to join them on the quarterdeck.

"Is there any indication about the time of day for the ritual to take place?"

"I didn't see any," Cariad said.

Harriet said, "The legends and myths I followed to find Granny Wise in the first place never indicated a time. Sunrise, dusk, it didn't matter when you found her. So I assume she could do it at any time of day." She looked at the sky. "For some reason it feels appropriate to do it at sunset, though."

"I agree," Clio said.

"Clio..." Harriet drew the name out as much as possible. "If you change your mind at any point~"

Clio held up a hand to cut her off. "None of that. I have no regrets, qualms, or reservations about this. You stuck your head in a noose to save this crew. I can put my mind at risk to keep you safe a while longer."

Harriet reached out and linked her fingers with her wife's.

Clio chose a small contingent to join them on the island, just Fausta, Ranzi, and Delfina, and they set out as soon as they were within the launch's range. Fausta rowed, while Cariad spent the trip skimming and re-reading the journal pages. At this point, Clio was confident that the girl had the spell memorized, but there wasn't any harm in chiseling the information into her brain now that they were so close to the moment of truth.

Once ashore, Cariad walked slowly with her head angled to the sand. She strayed away from the group, crouched down, and returned to them with a wide, flat stone. She held it out to Harriet, who took it and turned it over in her palm as if expecting to find a message written on it.

"Just any stone?" she said.

"There are some specifics, but we can alter it when we're ready to do the ritual."

Clio gestured at the rest of the small island, which was identical to where they stood. A flat stretch of sand and stone, a bit of scrub, and then open sea stretching out in every direction. She turned around to face them. "Here is as good as anywhere else."

Cariad shrugged. "Okay. Here works."

Delfina looked skeptical. "And you can just... *do* this? Granny Wise was... is... was... a witch. With powers, if you believe that sort of thing."

"Rituals and spells are a lot like recipes," Cariad said. "Granny Wise may have been an expert chef, but anyone with a kitchen could copy the same meals she did. I'm..." She gestured at herself. "I can cook well enough to follow instructions. Besides, Harriet's soul or consciousness is already somewhere it isn't supposed to be. It shouldn't take too much effort to convince it to move somewhere else. Our current situation is proof of how easily it can happen. Harriet went into Santiago's body on accident. It shouldn't be too hard to do it deliberately."

Clio said, "How do you ensure you've targeted the right, um, person? No offense to Santiago, but I don't want to end up with him in my head and Harriet stuck alone in his body."

"Oh, that won't happen," Cariad said. "I mean, he could attempt to hijack the swap. And Harriet's consciousness *would* take over the body if that happened. But the swap requires consent on both parties. Your mind will be focused on Harriet. If Santiago tried to come along, you could bounce him out."

"Into his own body?"

Cariad shrugged. "Into anything, really. Once the consciousness, or soul, or whatever is out of the body, it just needs a vessel. You could send it into the ether if you wanted."

Harriet said, "Don't send Santiago into the ether."

"I won't," Clio promised. "He's a very nice man."

Harriet grinned.

Delfina crossed her arms over her chest. She still looked skeptical, but didn't seem prepared to continue pressing.

Cariad put the journal on the ground and held it in place with her foot. She took a pen and inkwell from her pocket and held it out to Harriet. "You need to draw a design on the stone. It doesn't matter what the design is, as long as it's something you came up with on your own."

Harriet looked at Clio, then at the others around her. She shrugged and began to draw a nautical star. When she finished, she gave the pen back and blew on the ink to dry it.

"Captain Landau, you and... ah... C-Captain Landau should face each other." They moved into position.

Fausta snickered. "I feel like we're watching their wedding all over again."

"I wasn't there for that," Ranzi said.

"Oh, it's quite the story."

Clio said, "One for another time. Go ahead, Cariad."

She cleared her throat. "Well, it's fairly simple. Harriet, hold the stone in your hand. Clio, cover Harriet's hand with both of yours. Harriet, with your free hand, grip Clio's forearm. Clio, it is very important that you hold the image of Harriet in your mind. Not just her name. Her voice, her posture, those things that make her Harriet Landau."

Clio smiled. "I have them."

Harriet winked at her.

"Now, we have to be very careful about this. Santiago is the primary inhabitant of the body. If we start the process and Harriet tries to retreat, he could choose to block her way. She wouldn't be able to go back and then her spirit would disperse. No coming back from that. So we have to be very sure that Santiago is a willing participant here. If something goes wrong and Harriet has to go back..."

"He accepts," Harriet said.

"Why would she have to go back?" Clio asked.

Cariad shrugged. "We don't know how your mind will react to someone else trying to barge in. You might put up a wall to keep her out. I'm just saying it to be safe. I don't want to fuck this up."

"We appreciate it, Miss Baillie," Harriet said.

"Okay. Clio, the words you have to keep in mind are *Untether and arrive into me.* Harriet, your words are *I beseech you to grant me entrance.*"

Harriet said, "I didn't have to think anything when Granny Wise set the spell."

Cariad shrugged. "Well, I'm not as talented as a four hundred year old witch. Besides, putting a marque on someone is much different than hopping ship." She held up a hand. "Now please, this all seems very simple, but it's complicated and everything has to be perfectly aligned so the right person goes into the right body. Is everyone ready?"

She received murmured assents from all gathered.

"Okay. Now close your eyes." She looked at the witnesses. "That goes for everyone. Eyes closed."

The group did as instructed. Cariad reached into the back of her pants where she'd stowed a pistol. She held it over Clio's shoulder, aiming behind her, and squeezed her eyes shut.

She pulled the trigger.

Clio recoiled and barked a curse, releasing Harriet's hand as she lurched to the side. Harriet also dropped into a crouch, while Ranzi and Fausta both reached for their own weapons and searched for their attackers. Clio had dropped to her knees and was cradling her ear. Fausta had quickly spotted the smoking gun and crossed quickly to Cariad, grabbing her wrist with one hand while she closed the other around the writer's throat.

"The fuck was that?" Fausta hissed.

Cariad choked and dropped the gun. "It was... ne-necessary. And she couldn't know it was coming. Needed the..." She croaked and tried to wriggle free from Fausta's grip. "Shock."

"You're lucky we didn't shoot you," Ranzi growled, kneeling to check on Clio. Delfina had also rushed forward to examine the captain's ear.

"I can explain." Cariad tapped the back of Fausta's hand. "Need... to breathe, though."

Fausta released her, eyes dark.

Cariad coughed and rubbed her throat. "There needs to be a jolt. The brain needs to... t-to... well, Granny Wise used the word 'hiccup.' Harriet went into Santiago while he was having an orgasm. I assumed the captain wouldn't want to use that method out here in the open." She looked at Clio. "Captain? I'm sorry. I needed genuine shock and—"

"It's fine!" Clio's voice was just below a shout, and she still had her hand pressed against her ear. "I understand why you did it! I wish you'd come up with a different method, but given the rapidly-closing window you were given..."

"The important thing is that it worked," Santiago said.

Ranzi glanced at him, then snapped her head back to look again. Cariad was also startled by the changes in him. His hair was still long and knotted in a ponytail, but his posture was different. Moments ago it had been easy to forget he was male, but suddenly there was no mistaking his gender. He lifted his arm and revealed the tattoo which had appeared above his elbow after Harriet's resurrection had vanished without so much as a scar.

Ranzi slowly got to her feet as she examined him, then she looked down at Clio.

"Harriet?"

"I'm here." It sounded like Clio, but not. It was almost as if she was faking an accent. Harriet looked at Cariad. She held up her left arm to reveal a nautical star tattooed on the inside of her wrist. "The writer girly did it."

Delfina said, "And Clio?"

"Here as well," Clio said in her normal voice.

"Criminy," Fausta said. "That's going to be odd."

"Hopefully we won't have time to get used to it," Clio said as she got to her feet. "This is a time-saving decision, nothing more. This experiment didn't just save Santiago. It proved we no longer have to find the *Loyal Sea* to put an end to this madness. We don't need Granny Wise to save Harriet. We just need Miss Baillie here."

"And a body," Harriet interjected. "Yes, naturally. And a body," Clio said, seeming to agree with herself.

Fausta shook her head. "I may have to stop drinking until things get set right..."

Harriet laughed. "Probably not a bad idea, Miss Gittens. Come on, now. Let's get back to my~"

"~back to our ship," Clio said, her voice somehow layering with Harriet's in a way that no human throat should have been capable of.

She walked to the launch, leaving everyone else on the beach to stare after her.

CHAPTER FOURTEEN

OVER THE next few days, the crew began noticing oddities about their captain. Clio's eyes were brown, but after the ritual, the right one slowly faded until it became the blue of Harriet's. Her hair had been white silver but now there were threads of charcoal gray running through it. Sometimes she spoke with a slightly different inflection, a deeper tone, and it took some people a few seconds to realize the order had come from her.

Santiago Zeno couldn't get off the ship fast enough. They returned to Baleares immediately so he could recover on familiar ground. It seemed unlikely they would see him willingly return to the *Banshee* any time soon. By the time he left, everyone aboard had heard enough of what happened to have an opinion on it.

The trip to take Santiago home had taken two days. The night they left Baleares, Cariad joined a poker game taking place in the mess. Fausta brought the cards, Estacia had provided snacks, and the peanuts were being used as currency. As the game progressed, conversation turned to their captain's current situation and where they could possibly go after this development.

"She could use a dead body," Ranzi said, tossing a nut into the pot.

"That's disgusting," Cariad said, meeting her bet.

Ranzi shrugged. "Why? If it's not rotted yet, it should be fine."

"But it would start to rot eventually, right?" Cariad looked around the table, but no one looked to have an idea either way. "Just because the body has a consciousness inside it doesn't mean the body will keep working. Otherwise we could just carve a body out of wood."

"You're the one who read the book." Fausta added to the pot. "Does it say anything about putting someone into a corpse?"

"No," Cariad admitted. "I assumed it was more of an unspoken understanding. Some things are just... not done... even if you aren't religious."

Delfina folded. "Decomposition begins immediately after death. Even if... God, I can't believe I'm even entertaining this notion. Even if Harriet was put into a dead body, and even if her presence stopped the body from rotting, she would have to be swapped in *immediately* or else there would already be considerable damage."

"We really start decomposing immediately?" Cariad asked.

Delfina shrugged. "Pretty much."

Fausta said, "So Harriet would have to be present when the person died."

"And the death couldn't be natural," Delfina said. "If they succumbed to an illness, and Harriet revived it, the illness would still be there ready to start over."

Ranzi said, "So not just a dead body. A murdered body."

"Mm," Delfina said. "And murdered in a way that doesn't leave a mark. Shooting, stabbing, blood loss, broken neck... you wouldn't want to be in a broken body."

Fausta ended the hand on top and collected her winnings. "The way I see it," she said, dealing another hand, "the captains want something impossible. She won't take over a body someone is already using, at least not permanently. It's not as if there are loads of empty bodies waiting for someone to hop inside and take the helm."

Cariad said, "And even if Harriet was willing to share a body with someone, there's no guarantee she would have any control. She got lucky with Santiago, which I believe is due to his general passiveness. And Clio was obviously a willing host. So there seems to be some kind of balance there. But what if she gets stuck in someone like Isobel Ronan?"

"And what about Ronan?" Ranzi said. "Are we still chasing her down? I asked while we were on the way to take Santiago home, and Clio just said Ronan 'wasn't a priority' at the moment."

Cariad shrugged. "We were hunting her because of Granny Wise, so she could fix the Santiago situation. I guess when I figured out how to do it instead, the *Loyal Sea* became less important."

"Apparently things have been quiet since our last run-in," Ranzi said. "Maybe the crew is too weak to go after any more towns."

Fausta grunted and tossed some nuts into the pot. "We should probably do something eventually. We need those ports intact and well-stocked."

"And friendly to outsiders," Ranzi said.

"Mm," Fausta agreed, and folded her hand.

Estacia sat down next to Cariad, glancing at her cards. "So if we're not chasing Ronan and her crew, what exactly *are* we doing now?"

"Looking for work, as always," Fausta said. "We've lost a lot of time chasing after that witch. We might as well fill our coffers until she pops up again."

"I suppose that makes sense." Cariad touched Estacia's thigh under the table, giving it a squeeze. "I won't deny a few days of relative quiet sounds pretty nice to me."

Ranzi hissed through her teeth and wet her fingers in her drink. "Never say things like that on a ship, Baillie. Only brings bad omens." She flicked her fingers in Cariad's direction. "Anything bad happens, I'm blaming it on you."

"Fair enough. Does this count?" Cariad put her cards down. "Full house."

Ranzi slapped her own cards down and swore.

Despite Cariad's tempting of fate, the following week was indeed quiet and calm. They were spent a day in Palermo asking around for commissions, eventually getting hired to transport several crates of "sensitive cargo" to Dublin. At top speed, the trip would have taken six days, but the client didn't seem particularly rushed. Clio decided they would take their time.

They left the Mediterranean, passing through Gibraltar and heading north. They skirted a storm as they passed Portugal, and Cariad spent most of that day on-deck writing about the sights and sounds of a storm at sea. She was trying to describe the colors of distant rainfall, still stuck on how to convey the rumble of thunder as it crossed the water, when she became aware of someone standing next to her. She turned and saw Clio had joined her at the railing.

"Hello, Captain." The captain had spent most of the past few days in her cabin. When she did venture out, whether to get food or check their progress, she rarely said more than a few words to anyone she encountered. When it became clear she wasn't going to just move on, Cariad risked further conversation. "I'm not certain how to ask this but, ah, who are you?"

She smiled. "Harriet is the one currently steering the ship. Clio is taking a rest."

"How exactly does that work?" Cariad asked.

"I haven't the slightest idea," Harriet laughed. "It's madness. We seem to have found a balance to it. Sometimes one of us is in complete control, other times we're both... aware... and either of us could say or do whatever she wants. The best times are at night. When we're falling asleep. Neither of us is in control, the body is still, and we're just two minds." She sighed, smiling dreamily. "I never thought I'd... I never thought it would be possible to exist with someone this way."

Cariad couldn't help but smile at how happy Harriet sounded. "And there haven't been any further changes? Beyond the eye and your hair. I feel like by this time with Santiago, we had started seeing more drastic alterations to his body."

"None that I've noticed." Harriet stepped back and looked down at her body as if she expected to see a second pair of arms had sprouted somewhere. "Being the same sex probably made it easier. Clio is shorter than I am, but other than that we have similar builds. It might have saved us some of the more noticeable changes."

"I suppose that's lucky."

"Mm. When we do find someone for me to move permanently into, *if* we find that person, it definitely must be a woman."

Cariad shrugged. "You do have the rare experience of knowing what it's like to live as both."

Harriet nodded. "There are some, ah... hah... enticing parts of the male anatomy, but it's not somewhere I'd like to spend the rest of my days."

"Yes..." Cariad pressed her lips together. "There's also that."

"Mortality?"

"Right," Cariad said. "This supports the myth that Granny Wise has been around on the island for hundreds of years. There's no reason to think your life has to end with whatever body you end up taking. Hell, there's no reason any of us have to accept death as the end."

Harriet smiled. "You're making a very privileged assumption. You're imagining a scenario where one knows death is looming and can make plans. But me and the other women aboard this ship, yourself included, are all far more likely to die at the end of a sword. Fire or drowning, hung from the neck until dead, starved. There are a lot of ways we can end up dying. We don't have the luxury of planning or dying old. And it would be foolish to think a little magic would be the only thing required to give us immortality."

Cariad nodded. "I suppose that's a good point. It might also be why Granny Wise spent her life on the same island, hidden away."

"Quite possibly, yes. It's an interesting question. Would you choose to live forever if it meant hiding away like that? Experiencing the world only through the eyes of other people?"

"Oh, heavens no," Cariad said immediately. "I can't imagine anything more tedious than living forever, no matter the circumstances. I would rather have a life. Knowing it will end at some point makes it worthwhile. I feel like I've lived more in the year I've been on this ship than Granny Wise ever did."

Harriet smiled. "I would definitely agree with that, Miss Baillie."

Cariad looked at her. "You didn't call me 'the writer.' Or 'girly'."

"That would be disrespectful to a member of my crew." She winked and clapped Cariad on the shoulder. "I never would have allowed you on board, Cariad Baillie, but Clio's wisdom has proven I would've been wrong to keep you away."

"That means a lot to me, Harriet. Thank you."

"You're welcome. You know, I've... I write a little myself." She chuckled. "Clio just told me that she shared one of my poems with you."

Clio nodded. "Storms and ships called she. I liked it. I'd like to hear more, if you're willing to share."

Harriet nodded. "I'll see what I can dig up. In the meanwhile, is your lovely partner hard at work in the kitchen? I'm a bit famished."

"I think she can whip something up for you, if you asked nicely."

Harriet grinned and winked. "I'll see if I can manage nice."

Cariad absolutely adored Dublin. The *Banshee* spent five days there after completing their job. Everyone got a little time off the ship. Cariad took Estacia on a tour of the best restaurants in the city so she could experience "true Irish cuisine," while the rest of the crew spent their time ashore engaged in various other pursuits. Clio vanished immediately after they delivered their cargo and settled payment. Fausta was left in charge of any ship-related business and, as far as Cariad could tell, spent most of every day napping in a hammock on the deck.

When they finally set out again, they had received another commission and their hold was full of more mysterious cargo. Cariad didn't mind being kept in the dark on the specifics of their jobs. She didn't need or want to know the who, how, or what, as long as it kept Estacia well-paid and the kitchen stocked. A full pantry made Estacia happy, and a happy Estacia was all Cariad needed.

They were only a few hours out from Dublin when a thick fog rolled in. Tis Common had shouted a warning about it, but the bank was so vast that there was no choice but to continue on into the haze.

Cariad went up on deck to watch. She'd never been on a fogbound ship. There was something ethereal about it, as if they had traveled into another world. The ship slowed to a crawl. The waves slapping against the hull sounded much louder than usual. The fog veiled the sun and made everything gray-blue despite the fact it was early afternoon.

The deck was silent of its normal conversations. Cariad watched wisps of smoke curl around the sails, which were just barely being filled with wind, and shuddered.

"Glad this doesn't happen often," she said in a whisper, half to herself.

"Aye," a passing crewman agreed. "Always gives me the shivers..."

Cariad decided her time would be better spent below decks, reading or writing by lantern light, finally grateful for the fact there were no windows in her room.

She had just started below when she heard a shrill whistle. She stopped and turned back to look toward the quarterdeck. Normally that sound indicated Aravanis gathering the crew, but the large Greek woman was at the helm with both hands on the wheel. The whistle came again, and Aravanis tilted her head just enough to prove she'd heard the sound as well. Cariad returned to the deck and searched for the source of the whistle.

"Starboard bow!"

The cry came from Ranzi, who had climbed onto a barrel to get a better view. Her left arm was wrapped around the rigging, while her right was pointed straight out. Cariad looked where she was pointing and, if she strained, she thought she could see a dark shape moving through the fog bank. The ship suddenly took a hard turn to port and Cariad looked up to see Aravanis rapidly spinning the wheel to change their course.

"To your quarters!" The cry came from Captain Landau as she emerged from below. "All non-essential hands, get your asses off this deck!"

Cariad watched as people scrambled to follow her order, while others took position at the guns along the railing. Her heart pounded as the dark shape broke through the fog and seemed to aim itself right at them.

A year ago, she would have said one ship looked like any other. She wouldn't have been able to identify any particular vessel if she'd been standing on the deck staring at its name on the hull. But her time aboard the *Banshee* had taught her much, including the tiny characteristics that made every ship unique and easily distinguishable.

That was how she knew she was looking at the *Loyal Sea*.

"Bloody hell," she muttered.

Someone grabbed her collar and yanked her back, stopping her heart as she first believed they had somehow already been boarded. But the voice that barked in her ear belonged to Ranzi.

"You heard the captain, damn it! Get yourself down below!"

Ranzi let her go and ran toward the bow before Cariad could muster a response. The fog had closed around them so tightly that she couldn't see that part of the ship. She spun on the ball of her foot and looked toward the quarterdeck. Clio had taken the helm. Aravanis had disappeared somewhere. She wondered where Fausta was, and—

The first blow shook the entire structure of the *Banshee*, knocking Cariad off her feet. She was sent sprawling. Her journal flew from her hands but she somehow managed to grab it in mid-air, clutching it to her chest with one arm as she regained her footing. Wood creaked all around her. She heard the ripple of cloth from overhead and feared it was a loosened sail. She couldn't imagine what that might mean for them, but it seemed like a fatal loss if it wasn't addressed quickly.

Clio was shouting orders. Aravanis had reappeared loaded with weapons, guns and swords, which she pressed into the hands of anyone she passed. She spotted Cariad and narrowed her eyes, clearly wondering what the hell she was doing there. Cariad was wondering the same thing. She was turned around, dizzied by the chaos all around her, and she'd lost all her directions. She spotted the doorway she believed led to relative safety and ran for it.

She was nearly there when another blow lifted the deck. She managed to stay on her feet but was spun in a circle so she could see the spray of smoke and splintering wood from the impact. Something hit her in the forehead, a solid impact that splattered something warm and wet over her face. Her body slammed into the deck just as the pain registered in her skull, like the impact had cut a furrow straight through her brain.

Cariad was aware of sliding, of smoke and shouting, and someone running toward her. She thought she heard Fausta whisper, "Oh Jesus Christ," from above her.

And then the world went dark...

...and the battle must have ended...

...because everything after was silence.

CHAPTER FIFTEEN

STRANGE...

Strange, to wake in bed but feel so exhausted. Strange to hear voices but lack the ability to understand the words. To tell your eyes to open and be ignored. Cariad felt her head, although it was more like a big bag of air, and she felt her right arm and both her legs below the knee, both throbbing strangely. She felt every connected point between them and took comfort in the fact they felt relatively normal.

Her head seemed to be inside a pillowcase, which didn't make any sense. She reached up to correct the error before Estacia saw and made fun of her. Her right arm barely came off the mattress before dropping back into place. She whimpered, frustrated. Her eyes still weren't open. The pillowcase was squeezing her head. It hurt terribly.

"Miss Baillie?" Delfina. The doctor. She put her hand on Cariad's arm, then touched her cheek. Her palm was like ice. "Don't try to move, dear. Just relax."

"Tay...sha..."

She was so startled by how broken the name was on her tongue that she nearly didn't hear Delfina's response.

"Estacia is fine. She wasn't hurt. She's asleep right now."

"Don't wake her."

Delfina said, "Okay."

Cariad finally managed to get her left eye open halfway. She looked at Delfina, then past her at the other beds in the infirmary. So many beds, all of them full of people in agony. Arms and legs replaced with stumps wrapped in bloody bandages. Women with bloody blouses, their wounds being stitched by other crewmembers who, as far as Cariad knew, had no medical training.

"Oh no," she said, her voice feeling marginally stronger. "No, I'm... why are you wasting a bed on me..."

She started to push herself up, but Delfina pushed her back down. The woman was suddenly inhumanly strong, her hands like concrete slabs that Cariad couldn't hope to fight against.

"Why are you so strong?"

"Because you're very weak right now, Miss Baillie. You need more rest."

"These people are hurt badly," Cariad said. "I can rest in my own bed."

"Miss Baillie..." Delfina sighed. "Cariad. Please. You..."

She failed to find words. Instead, she reached for something on the bedside table. Cariad couldn't see what it was because her stubborn eye still refused to open. Delfina held the object up in front of her. A mirror, reflecting her face back to her.

Or rather, half her face.

The other half was swathed in bandages. Her left eye, the one that was actually working, was sunken in a deep pit of black bruises that spread out almost to her temple. A V-shaped line of stitches curled along her hairline above her left eyebrow. The skin around it looked hideous and dead. Her skin was pale, her lips dry.

"What..."

"You were hit with a piece of debris," Delfina said gently. "Fausta... y-you had... there was a..." She gestured near the side of her own head. "There was a piece of wood. In your eye."

Cariad inhaled sharply. "What?"

"I'm so sorry, Cariad. The eye is gone."

Cariad didn't understand. "How can it be gone?" She tried to open it to prove the doctor wrong, but the bandage was in the way. She lifted her hand again, and this time she actually managed to reach the tape holding the gauze in place. Delfina gently pulled her fingers away before she could pull it loose.

"I managed to clean the wound. And patch you up. You were very fortunate that Fausta found you immediately."

Her entire body was cold. She couldn't breathe, and she realized she was trembling.

"You're wrong," she said.

"Cariad, I'm sorry."

She wanted to yell, to scream for Delfina to give her eye back, though even in her current state she knew that was madness. Then the doctor was saying her name again, holding her shoulders, and Cariad only realized she was passing out as she was gently laid back on the pillow.

Clio stood in the rain and wind with Harriet. The starboard side of the ship was shattered. Their sails were ragged. There were holes in the deck that couldn't be patched. Four crewmembers had fallen overboard, lost to the churning waves as they fled from the attack. She supposed that meant everyone who remained onboard were the lucky ones, but that seemed to ignore the horrors they'd experienced. She wanted to say they had somehow outran the *Loyal Sea*, lost her in the fog, somehow slipped through Ronan's net, but she didn't believe that.

The only reason the *Banshee* was still intact was because Isobel Ronan let them go. She couldn't fathom why, or if they were just being toyed with.

Whatever the truth was, they had been badly and brutally beaten.

The attack had been three days ago. They were currently limping toward Portsmouth at a snail's pace. The repairs they needed could be done there, though God only knew how long it would take. They would be forced to cancel their commission from Dublin and pass the cargo off to another ship. It would be a devastating blow to their coffers, combined with paying for the repairs.

"You came back just in time to see me destroy your ship," Clio muttered.

"There was nothing you could have done," Harriet said in the same dry, cracked voice.

"And that is supposed to be a comfort? To make me feel helpless?"

Harriet had no retort for that. Clio crossed her arms over her chest. Her right arm drifted up and stroked her cheek gently. She closed her eyes and turned her head away from the caress.

"Stop it."

"Do you remember what I've always said?" Harriet touched Clio's cheek again. "Nothing is a complete failure. The day I died, my crew escaped. And the day we were ambushed by a brutal enemy, the majority of our crew survived."

Clio shook her head. "I can't look at any of this as a positive, Harriet. We could be completely ruined by this. Maybe that was Ronan's intention. Death is one thing, but ruination... that's probably *fun* for her. She'll probably hunt us down when we're all beggars and spit in our collecting cups."

Harriet sighed. "I wish I could still walk away from you when you get like this. Sometimes you just needed space to get your bad thoughts out. But since I'm stuck here listening to it, I'm going to try fixing it. If it's at all within my power."

"Bring me the head of Isobel Ronan. And her ship. And then... maybe... I can begin to move on. But beyond that..."

"We will find her. Not today, and maybe not even soon. But she will pay for what she's done to our ship. You have my vow on that."

Clio managed a smile. "You always did find ways to keep your vows."

"Exactly. I once said I'd never leave you, and look how far I've gone to keep that promise."

Clio laughed.

"I'm glad you find something about this amusing."

Clio and Harriet turned to see Fausta had joined them. Her arm was still bound to her torso with a tightly-wrapped cloth, but she was holding a sheaf of papers. Harriet retreated and Clio felt herself moving to center, taking control. The damage report immediately after the battle had been grim. Nothing that would cause them to take on water, thank whatever fates were watching over them. But the starboard side had been beaten full of holes, and the mizzenmast sail hung in limp tatters. Fausta had spent the past few days doing a full accounting of the cost, and the look on her face was not encouraging.

Fausta didn't waste time softening the blow. "We'll be at least a month in Portsmouth." She looked down at the decimate bulwark. One false step, one unexpected wave, and they could lose another crewmember. "And even if we cash in every favor we have, it's going to cost most of what we've got just to get her back in fighting shape."

Clio swore under her breath. "Nothing to be done about

either, I suppose. I'm glad we've got the coin to be spent. What of the injured crew?"

Fausta drew in a breath in let it out slowly. "Healing. Slowly. Delfina is run ragged trying to care for all of them, but she's wrangling up helpers whenever she can." She paused. "Miss Baillie woke up."

"Oh god. How is she coping?"

"She immediately passed out after Delfina told her what happened. I can't say as I blame her. Estacia is with her again. Kicking herself something fierce for not being there when she woke up."

Clio said, "Remind her that she's needed in the mess. The rest of the crew still need to eat."

"I'll remind her. Compassionately, if I can."

"Much obliged."

Fausta remained, then finally said what was on her mind. "The fuck did she attack us for? We're not even hunting her down, not causing her any trouble. Had no idea she was even out here now."

Clio said, "I think she's afraid we know too much about her. Granny Wise, her crew, all of it. The fact she's out here now, and so powerful, makes me worry she's stronger than before. If she's intent on destroying us, we may not have the ability to fight back. Let alone come out of it victorious."

"That doesn't sound like you, Captain."

"We don't have much of a choice," Clio said. "We're close to losing everything anyway. The best course of action might be to just split up what we have left in the coffers and let everyone disperse. They'll find other ships, they'll... they'll..."

Fausta was staring at her like she was an alien. Clio started to say something further, but she pressed her lips together and set her jaw. The overwhelming feeling of resignation was eclipsed by a sudden righteous anger.

"No. We will *not* run. No person on this ship is prey, certainly not to a vulture like Isobel Ronan. We'll take the time to lick our wounds and get back on our feet. We'll repair our ship... our *home*. And then we'll take the fight to her."

"Aye, captain," Fausta said, grinning widely. "Had me worried there for a second."

Clio grunted. "Me too."

When Fausta had left, Clio walked toward the stern. The fog had long since dissipated, but there was still a heavy cloud cover that made it feel as if they were sailing under a blanket.

"That was you, wasn't it?" she said under her breath.

"What do you mean?" Harriet asked.

Clio scoffed and shook her head. "You could never play innocent when you were alive. Why in the world would you try *now*? Those words coming out of my mouth, that dark and dour mood closing in around everything. I've never felt that defeated. I just wanted to curl up and..." She blinked hard and looked down. "You... felt like that a lot, didn't you?"

Harriet remained silent.

"The quiet days," Clio said. "The days when you stayed in our cabin to plot a course. I thought you just trusted me to run the ship-"

"I did, love."

"-but you... you couldn't do it on those days. God, Harriet, why didn't you say anything?"

Harriet lifted her head and blinked away tears. "There was nothing you could have done that you weren't already doing. I didn't want you to look down on me. To see me as lesser."

Clio brushed the back of her hand over her cheek. "I know you didn't have a choice this time, but thank you for showing that part of yourself to me. I'm sorry I never saw it before."

"I hid it well. Behind anger, behind lashing out at you for small things so you'd put some distance between us. It's harder to suppress like this. You did an excellent job pushing it back."

"Thank you. I'll keep an eye out for it in the future. You don't have to fight it alone anymore, love."

She felt warmth pass through her chest and knew, somehow, Harriet had just given her a hug. She smiled and looked out at the sea. Isobel Ronan could break their ship, but they would never be broken.

They would recover from this. And the *Loyal Sea* would know the true rage of banshees.

CHAPTER SIXTEEN

THE REPAIRS to the *Banshee* ended up taking nine weeks.

As soon as they arrived in Portsmouth, Fausta arranged passage on another ship so she could set out and learn as much as possible about the *Loyal Sea* and Isobel Ronan. Ranzi and Aravanis contacted carpenters and shipbuilders who would oversee the repairs to the ship, calling in favors and negotiating prices so it wouldn't cost them everything just to stay afloat. The Captains Landau found a room within view of the harbor, so they would never be very far away from their ship if an issue arose.

Most of the crew either signed up with the carpenters to help repair the *Banshee* or found work in and around Portsmouth for the duration they'd be grounded. Estacia was quickly hired as a cook at the alehouse near the docks and used the funds from her meager first paycheck to rent a room on the landward side of town.

Cariad spent most of her time in bed. She was still getting used to her new, bizarre world of only having one eye. When she'd finally been released from the infirmary, the right side of her head was still bandaged. She insisted on making her own way back to the cabin she and Estacia had been sharing. She would have to learn to move around the ship without an escort sooner or later, and she would much rather get started.

Her victory was tarnished when she arrived to find Estacia in the midst of emptying out the nightstand on her side of the bed.

"Are you kicking me out?" Cariad asked, panic rising in her chest.

"What?" Estacia looked at her, then looked at the pile on the bed. "Oh! N-no, no, no." She laughed and gestured at the mattress. "I was swapping. Your side and my side. Because... your right eye... um..." She looked suddenly unsure of herself. "I thought, um. You sleep on the port side of the bed. And with your eye, I th-thought that would mean you could only see me if you rolled all the way over onto your right side. This way, you'll be on the starboard. And you can see me to your left no matter if you're on your back or-or..." She grunted and pushed a hand into her hair. "I'm sorry. I should have asked. I-I'll put everything back."

"Don't. Don't." Cariad came into the room. She cupped Estacia's face and lifted it, kissing her softly and then with more passion. "I love you for thinking of that."

"I almost lost you. I don't want you to spend a second trying to find me when you wake up."

Cariad smiled and kissed her again.

Now, in Portsmouth, the bandage had been replaced by a padded triangle of white leather. The strap stretched around her head like a small belt. Estacia was required to secure the catch every morning, since it rested at the back of Cariad's skull under her hair. The first few days, Cariad apologized to her for the inconvenience. Estacia had just embraced her from behind and kissed her neck, then assured her she would do it "every morning, every night, and any other time in between."

She felt useless. It was difficult to focus on anything for very long. Reading or writing too long nauseated her. She got dizzy. She had become clumsy. She couldn't even tidy their room because it was too small to get messy. And because she couldn't trust herself to walk around without falling, she had to rely on Estacia's income to keep her fed and housed. It was humiliating, and it was devastating to know there was nothing she could do to fix it.

They had been grounded for two weeks. She'd spent most of that time in bed. Today, however, she was going to change that. She opened the drawer and took out the gift Delfina had delivered to her a few days earlier: a pair of eyeglasses with the right lens whited out. It would look odd, but hopefully less odd than the patch. She tried them on to make sure the left lens was correct for her vision.

She couldn't risk straining the one eye she had left. The thought of being completely blind ran cold water down her spine.

Cariad dressed and headed out. She didn't know where she was going. She just wanted to be out, to navigate the city under her own power without relying on anyone else.

Her adventure started out horribly when she tripped over the front step outside their lodging house. She swore under her breath, fought the urge to surrender and go back inside, and kept walking.

It wasn't long before she realized her feet were taking her to the docks. She could see the tall mast of the ships swaying in the harbor, sails neatly tucked away. They all combined into fenceposts from this distance, so she couldn't tell which one belonged to the place she'd been calling home these past few months. Of course, that might have been due to her injury. Everything seemed flat. She could tell everything had depth, to a degree. She could reach for things and grabbed them on the first attempt almost every time. But longer distances tended to look like backdrops from a theatre more than the real world. She didn't know if that would be permanent, or if she would adjust, but she felt like it was a question that could wait until later.

She stopped walking when she was close enough to see the ship. The work of the carpenters echoed up the streets, telling her that the *Banshee* was slowly coming back together. People were climbing all over the hull, secured by ropes and complicated pulley systems. She heard them shouting orders to each other but the individual words were pulled apart by the wind. A hand came to rest on her left shoulder, lightly enough that Cariad didn't jump before she turned to see Ranzi coming up beside her.

"Thank you for not sneaking up on me," Cariad said.

"I've known a few folks in your situation," Ranzi said. "Takes them some time to get used to it. But it also takes everyone else some time to get used to it. Don't hold it against anyone who just slips into your blind spot and starts talking, hm? They're not being cruel. It just means they see you as *you*, not the patch."

"I'll try to keep that in mind." She embraced herself. "You're not supervising the repairs?"

"Aravanis is taking care of that. Doing a cracker job, too. She's scaring the new hires far too much for them to even think about trying to take advantage of us."

"Does anyone ever stop being scared of Aravanis?"

Ranzi said, "Hard to say. I've only sailed with her for a couple of years." She winked and nudged Cariad with her elbow. "You doing all right, Baillie? Handling it well?"

Cariad grunted. "I don't have an answer to that."

"Fair. Fair." She crossed her arms as well, matching Cariad's posture. "A lot of us saw you that day. Fausta carrying you below decks. Your whole head was covered in blood. We thought..." She made a face. "You don't want to hear about all that. But if anyone acts queer around you, know that we *all* prefer having you with an eyepatch to... the alternative that we thought had happened. You savvy?"

Cariad was surprisingly touched. Her remaining tear duct stung with tears. She nodded, not trusting her voice.

Ranzi patted her shoulder again ."I've got to get back. Some of the crew are meeting at that tavern tonight for dinner." She pointed. "We've love to have ya. And I'm sure Estacia would like to eat food she didn't have to prepare for a change."

"I think she'd enjoy that quite a bit, actually."

"Eight o'clock. We'll save a seat for you both."

Cariad remained on the corner long after Ranzi left. There was a bench outside a building she eventually discovered was a barbershop and watched people arrive scruffy and leave polished. Seeing them transform was like magic. She quickly lost track of the time and had to hurry home as the sun was setting.

Estacia was already home when she arrived. She was sitting on the foot of the bed, in the middle of untying her boots. She looked up and smiled.

"Hi. I was hoping you'd gone for a walk."

"I didn't get far," Cariad admitted as she sat next to her partner. "I just went down to the docks so I could watch them work on the ship."

"How is it coming along?"

Cariad shrugged. "I spent more time in here." She tapped her temple. "Mind wandering."

"Oh? Anything interesting?"

Cariad pressed her lips together and furrowed her brow. She scratched the skin below her eyepatch, wondering if she should confess to what she'd really been thinking. Estacia could read her well enough at this point that she might as well have been shouting her conflict, so she decided there was no point in lying.

"I was thinking that given everything we're dealing with right now... Isobel Ronan, the Captains Landau, Granny Wise... there's no reason this~" She gesture to her eye. "~needs to be the thing you have to get used to. I could find a new body. A complete body. And then I could~"

"No," Estacia snapped.

"We could find someone you approve of, physically. That's~"

"No!" Estacia interrupted again, rising to stand in front of Cariad. "I'm sorry. I know it's your body so if you decide you need to do that, I-I-I won't stand in the way. But you said that *I* have to get used to. Cariad, love, do you think I care about one eye?" She dropped to her knees and took Cariad's hands in her own. "Compared to your smile? Or your ears?" She chuckled softly. "Or the way your hands feel in mine, or how-how-how you hold me at night? Your arms. *These* arms. No one else has these arms, or these fingers. No one else has your voice. Your laugh. I don't care about your eye. I care that you are here, alive."

Cariad's eye burned with tears. She felt a sharp tingling where her other eye had once been, but no tears fell from that side.

Estacia cleared her throat. "But. If you do decide to... do that. It's within your power. And I would understand. I know that no matter what you look like on the outside, you'll still be my Cariad. Even if you're missing an eye or wearing a different face."

Cariad sniffled and cupped Estacia's cheek. "I believe I shall keep this one for now."

"Good," Estacia said, rising up just enough to straddle Cariad's lap. "I am *quite* fond of it."

Cariad put her hands in the small of Estacia's back and accepted her kiss, whimpering with the lightest of protests as she was pushed down onto the mattress.

"R-Ranzi invited us to dinner..."

"When?" Estacia asked, moving her hand down to pluck at the buttons of Cariad's blouse.

Cariad tried to remember. "Um. Eight."

Estacia lifted her head to look at the clock. She nodded, and then slid down Cariad's body. "We have time." She unbuttoned Cariad's pants. "Or we'll be late. Either way..."

Cariad settled back and closed her eyes.

Either way.

Clio was standing at the window when Harriet woke up. It was an odd feeling. Similar to having an idea, but also like opening all the curtains to discover it was high noon outside.

"Good morning," Clio said. "You slept late today."

"I was up late," Harriet said, scanning the ship outside. "Looks like they're making solid progress. We may be back in business ahead of schedule."

"Perhaps," Clio said. "But I'm not rushing them. I want to be solid as steel before we face Ronan again. We'll be prepared."

Harriet made a noise of affirmation. "Any word from Fausta?"

Clio shook her head. "I wouldn't expect anything so soon. People might be afraid of talking. She may have already gained a reputation for vengeance."

"I've heard whispers."

"Oh you have? When?"

Harriet hesitated. "Last night. I couldn't sleep, so I went to the tavern."

"Aha! So that's why I felt hungover this morning."

"Apologies."

Clio waved it off. "We'll need to come to some sort of understanding, however. It's awkward for one of us to run around while the other is unaware."

"Agreed." Harriet slid her hand across Clio's stomach. "So what did you get up to while I was sleeping off my buzz?"

Clio looked down at the hand, watching as it teased the waistband of her trousers. "I stayed in. I read that book we got from the library. It was quite good."

"Is that so?" The button of the pants was undone, and Harriet slid her hand inside. "What was it about?"

"Oh it's quite good. Very funny. A, um... a sailor..." She cleared her throat as Harriet's hand cupped her within her pants. "A sailor is shipwrecked on an island inhabited by... v-very small... people." Harriet's fingers began moving against her. Clio drew in a sharp breath and slumped against the wall next to the window.

She cupped her own breast through her shirt, but the feeling faded from her hand as Harriet took control and gently caressed her. She sighed and imagined she was wrapped in Harriet's arms. She could almost feel her wife's solidness behind her. She rested her weight against the wall and imagined it was Harriet instead. Harriet's fingers teased her nipple and moved along the length of her sex.

"Tell me more about the book," Harriet whispered, her voice wavering with Clio's arousal.

"I can't remember..."

"I think you're lying," Harriet laughed, then moaned. "Oh, I miss kissing you…"

Clio wet her lips and surrendered more of her body to Harriet's roaming hands. Her mind swam. "This is so odd. I feel you."

"I feel you, too," Harriet whispered.

They undressed as they walked to the bed, climbing onto the mattress. Clio reached for the pillow and straddled it, gasping as she squeezed her thighs around the cotton. She bit her lip and rocked herself against it. She imagined she was rubbing herself against Harriet's thigh. She felt as if she could hear Harriet's moans in her head. She could hear her voice plain as day, murmuring encouragement even as Clio moaned in her own voice.

She came quickly, shuddering and stretching a hand out to the headboard as she fell forward. She caught her breath, eyes closed, lips parted.

"That was fun," Harriet said.

Clio laughed and wiped her hand across the sweat beading on her forehead. "Quite."

There was a pause. "I hope you don't think you're hiding that thought from me."

Clio's smile wavered. "This situation is familiar enough by now," she said. "I know I can't hide anything from you." She moved the pillow and flipped over onto her back. She laced her fingers together on her stomach and stared up at the ceiling. "I'm sorry for thinking it."

"You don't have to apologize for thinking," Harriet said. "Everyone has a right to their own private thoughts. I should apologize for listening in."

"It's not like you have a choice."

Harriet made a soft sound of agreement. "And the thought *is* true. As fun as that was, it's much more fun when we each have our own bodies."

"Not that I mind sharing an orgasm."

Harriet laughed. "That is quite a unique experience." She brushed the back of her hand over Clio's stomach. "We'll figure something out, love. One way or another."

"I know we will," Clio said.

This time she didn't try to hide her doubt and uncertainty and, to her credit, Harriet didn't bring it up.

CHAPTER SEVENTEEN

FAUSTA STRODE down the gangplank, her pack slung over her shoulder, her head turned to look at the *Banshee* so she could clock the progress of its repairs. The hull looked completely intact and mostly repainted. It honestly could have used a new paint job years ago. But now she looked battle-ready again. It was a relief; she had spent that same time on the *Resilience* finding out everything she could about the *Loyal Sea*. She hoped the crew would be found in equal condition to the ship. They'd had almost two months to rest, recuperate, and get ready to take the fight to Isobel Ronan. They were going to need it.

The first crewmember Fausta found was Ranzi, who greeted her with a crushing hug and a slap to the shoulder hard enough to knock the wind out of her. She recruited Ranzi to gather everyone else she could find and arranged a time for them to all gather together.

An hour later, Fausta was standing in front of the command crew in the back of the tavern. Clio and Harriet had welcomed her back and seemed particularly anxious about what she had to report. She was particularly glad to see Cariad Baillie seemed to be adjusting well to the loss of her eye. She'd been certain the girl was dead when she found her on the deck. A chunk of wood had been attached to her face, and her entire head dripped blood. The fact she was alive at all was a minor miracle.

Fausta had kept meticulous notes and flipped it open to scan what she'd written. She had the information memorized but desperately wanted to buy some time before she had to reveal it to the others. She cleared her throat and checked to make sure everyone was listening. Then she spoke.

"We're fucked. Simply put." She cleared her throat again, coughed into her fist. "Some time after we last encountered Captain Ronan, she sailed to Morocco. She found a crew which had recently lost its captain and offered her services. She told them she had magics to give them a lifetime's worth of sailing knowledge, skill, experience... They jumped at it, of course. But of course, it was a lie. She just transferred her loyal crewmembers into the new bodies and abandoned the starving, weakened shells.

"The *Loyal Sea* is now crewed by strong, young men with the knowledge of sailors who have spent their lives working together on ships. They are smart and coordinated. They are cruel. Brutal. Their attack on Skala was amateur. Scattershot. It was the flailing of dying people. But they're smarter now. Their attacks are focused, like the tip of a rapier. The *Banshee* isn't the only ship they've attacked. They don't even board or loot... they just slash our hamstrings and leave us to drown."

Clio worked her jaw, narrowed her eyes. "Where is the bitch now?"

"Portugal," Fausta said. "Not sure exactly where, but I have some leads. If we follow the coast we're bound to run into her 'fore long."

Clio turned to Aravanis. "When will the *Banshee* be ready to set sail?"

"Tomorrow."

"Really?" Clio said.

Ranzi nodded her agreement. "There's still things need done. But it's nothing that will affect our ability to defend ourselves. And it's nothing we can't do while at sea. I'd rather get after her now."

"Agreed," Fausta said.

There was a murmur of agreement from the rest of the group.

Delfina said, "I think we've all had enough resting and relaxing to last us a while. That ship is our home. She almost took it from us. I say we're all eager to show her a thing or two."

The murmur this time was louder.

"Bitch owes me an eye," Cariad said, just barely loud enough to hear.

Clio nodded to her and stood. "Then it's settled. Spread the word to anyone else who has taken up lodging in town. It's time to pack up before we start growing roots."

The crew filed out of the room, but Cariad stepped into Clio's path to stop her from joining the exodus. She cleared her throat and looked at the last of the crowd, indicating she wanted to say something privately. Clio acknowledged that and stood with her, silent, arms crossed over her chest. Once they were alone, she spoke softly.

"How fare you, Miss Baillie? No one would hold it against you if you would prefer to remain here for the duration."

"What? No. Like I said, I look forward to another encounter with this woman. I was actually going to ask about *your* situation."

Clio smiled. "Ah. We've gotten a bit more accustomed to sharing a body. Have you learned anything new from Granny Wise's journal?"

"I've read a bit more," Cariad said, "but deciphering her handwriting was difficult even before... And now I get headaches if I focus on any writing for too long, especially her scratching. But I'm trying, a little every day. She never attempted long-term swaps except for when she intended to stay in a body forever. So there's no record of what happens if a... if... someone stays inside another body for too long. There might be a time when it becomes irreversible."

Harriet furrowed her brow. "I don't understand. Why wouldn't you be able to just pop me out the same way you put me in?"

"Because it's... it's... like ice water, I suppose. When the transfer first occurred, it's like dropping an ice cube into a cup of water. For a few minutes you could still reach in and pluck the cube out. The cup is unchanged, the cube is the same, nothing to it. But if you wait, the cube begins to melt. Begins to... to... to blend." She looked at the two colors of Clio's eyes, indicating both Landaus were watching her. "It's the same concern we had when she was in Santiago's body. I don't think this is viable as a permanent solution."

"We'll consider that, Miss Baillie," Clio said. "Thank you for your counsel."

"If I can say one more thing?" Cariad held up her hands. "Estacia and I discussed the possibility of using the ritual on myself.

On a new body. For…" She gestured at her eye. "She was horrified by the thought. Because even though I might technically be whole again, I wouldn't be myself. I think you need to consider whether this, living like this, is really having Harriet back."

"I'm here," Harriet said, her voice small. "It's me, I'm…"

"Alive?" Cariad finished for her. "I don't know, honestly. But what if one day you wake up and Clio is quieter than normal? Or your hair has changed to Harriet's? Santiago was slowly being erased even though he seemed quite amenable to being a host. A human body isn't meant to be shared."

Clio looked down at her hands.

"It's all guesswork on my part," Cariad admitted. "And if you do decide to carry on like this, I completely understand. But I also think maybe this was never meant to be permanent. Maybe this was just a way to give you a chance to say a proper goodbye."

"Thank you for your insight, Miss Baillie."

Cariad nodded and awkwardly excused herself, leaving Clio and Harriet alone in the tavern's back room. Harriet rubbed the back of her neck. Clio meandered back toward the tables.

"Do you think she has a point?" Clio asked.

Harriet shrugged. "It's nothing we haven't discussed while we've been stranded here. I thought we'd come to an underst~"

"~anding, yes," Clio said, her voice somehow overlapping Harriet's. "But I can sense you aren't entirely convinced our current balance will continue. I feel it so I know you have as well. Some mornings it takes you longer to wake up. Your voice is becoming more like mine. Our eyes used to be two different colors, now they're blended."

"Like Miss Baillie's ice water."

"Exactly."

"We got complacent. Over two months. Things still seemed… fine. I didn't want to think about…" Clio pressed her lips together. "I don't want you to fade away."

"And I would be devastated if I forced you into… into hibernation, or God forbid something worse. I don't want to be resurrected at anyone's expense. Especially not yours. Perhaps that's why we've been having such difficulty thinking of a permanent solution…"

"…why we were so quick to accept this as an acceptable situation." Clio smoothed a hand over her blouse. "There *is* no moral answer. No way to give you a body without taking one."

Harriet was silent.

"So that's it?" Clio said. "I get this miracle and I have to accept it only lasts for... for a few weeks? I can only have you back permanently if I'm willing to risk my own consciousness?" Her eyes burned with tears. "It's not fair."

Harriet wiped away the tears with her knuckles. "I know, love. But Cariad may have been correct about another thing. I died far from you. Alone, at the hands of an enemy. Maybe the purpose of this miracle really is as simple as goodbye."

Clio kissed the wetness from the back of Harriet's hand. "I thought I said goodbye to you long ago. It shouldn't hurt so badly this time."

Harriet chuckled sadly. "I don't think it works that way, my love."

Clio wrapped her arms around herself and closed her eyes. She squeezed tightly, unsure if she was using her arms to hug Harriet's body, or if Harriet was hugging her. It didn't matter.

She just held on tightly and swayed to music only they could hear.

"Hey..."

Cariad jumped. She was at the desk in their room, hunkered over Granny Wise's journal with a lantern close enough for the flame within to be a threat to the page. She twisted around to see Estacia pushing the blankets away.

"No, no, stay in bed. I'm sorry. I thought the lantern was low enough..." She reached to lower the light further.

"Don't. It's bad enough for your eye trying to read in good light." Estacia got out of bed and rubbed her eyes as she crossed to the desk. "What are you doing?"

Cariad sighed. "I'm trying to find something useful in this damn book. We're setting sail tomorrow. We've never really come out on top against Isobel Ronan. I'm worried we might just be running to a bloodbath. I thought maybe if this journal has something as miraculous as bringing people back from the dead, then maybe there's something else that could be useful."

Estacia gently massaged Cariad's temples. "Have you found anything?"

"Nothing." Cariad sighed. "She has many other spells and rituals, but they're mostly useless to us. This one..." She flipped back a few pages. "It helps a garden grow faster, even in winter. It would be very helpful to farmers, but not much help to people living at sea. Ah, and here." She moved her finger down the page. "It can make a pinecone taste like an apple."

"That could be helpful if you were stranded on a desert island."

"A desert island with pine trees?"

Estacia giggled. "I don't know. It could happen."

"The massage feels great, by the way. Thank you."

"You're welcome." She bent down and kissed the top of Cariad's head. "Captain Landau has always found a way to beat impossible odds. You saw what happened on your first trip with us. She defeated an all-powerful witch! She took down an entire invisible island."

Cariad sighed. "Part of me wishes we had succeeded with that mission. The ability to become invisible would be amazingly helpful at the moment." She idly flipped through a few pages. "Granny Wise just never saw the need for defensive or offensive magic of any sort. Nothing to help in a fight, nothing to give someone an advantage against another ship."

Estacia looked at the pages over Cariad's shoulder. "There has to be something useful in there. It doesn't have to explicitly be a weapon, you know. Anything can be used to inflict harm on an enemy. Or to gain the upper hand in a fight. You just have to adapt it to your needs. Like Jesus, yes? Water into wine. A very good thing at a dinner party, but not helpful if you're on a ship at sea with thirsty sailors."

"That's a clever way of looking at it, love." Cariad kept flipping pages. "I don't know if there's anything like that in here, though. Or maybe I just don't have the right brain to figure out how to twist these blessings to become burdens. Maybe you could look through it."

"Mm, I am too tired. And I don't read English very well."

"You don't?" Cariad looked up at her. "You read what I write all the time."

Estacia shrugged. "That's worth the effort. And I can ask you to help when I need a word." She stroked Cariad's hair. "Come to bed, love. You tried. If there is nothing that can help, it won't do anyone any good to have you exhaust yourself like this."

Cariad sighed and shut the book. "You're right. Even if I did find something that could be twisted into a useful spell, we would have to be very close to implement it." She held her hand out and Cariad took it, allowed herself to be pulled up and led back to bed.

"I just feel like I'm missing something. Like someone smarter than me or with more sailing experience could see it."

She sighed and sat down on her new side of the bed. She had gotten used to it quickly, and every morning she made a point to wait until she was facing Estacia before she opened her eye.

"You are a brilliant woman," Estacia said, settling in against her pillow. "If there was something that might help, I know you would have found it. Granny Wise wanted to help people. She wanted to grant their wishes. Turning straw into gold is just not very useful in a fight."

"Hah," Cariad chuckled softly. "You joke, but there actually is a spell that..." Her voice trailed off as her brain darted away. "And... it could be implemented..."

Estacia sat up again. "Love...?"

Cariad stood up quickly. She grabbed her robe and shoved her arms into the sleeves, already moving toward the bedroom door.

"I have to go find the captains."

"It's the middle of the night."

Cariad smiled back at her. "This is worth waking up for. Thank you, Estacia. You may have just given the *Banshee* exactly what it needs to defeat Isobel Ronan."

CHAPTER EIGHTEEN

THE BANSHEE set sail again the following day at dawn. A few people elected to remain behind at Portsmouth, but they had more than enough crew for their mission. Clio was at the helm, with Cariad beside her. Fausta had gotten a few leads on where they were most likely to find Ronan and her new barbarians. She'd spent the past month terrorizing Portugal but rumor had it she'd moved north into the Bay of Biscay, aiming to strike any Spanish galleons that might cross her path.

Once they were away from shore, Clio looked at Cariad. "You're certain this ritual of yours works over a long distance?"

"The book explicitly says it can be used to affect villages across entire islands. I looked again this morning. It won't affect us but, as long as we're within eyesight of the *Loyal Sea*, it will work."

Harriet said, "It will be a damn short fight if it turns out you're wrong."

"I've been through this entire journal," Cariad said, hoping she sounded more certain than she felt. "This is the only thing that sounds remotely useful. I think it will work."

"And you have everything you need?" Clio asked.

Cariad nodded. "I'll be ready."

"Good girl," Harriet said. "Even at top speed, it will be

tomorrow before we're anywhere near close enough to Spain. But we've got Tis Common in the crow's nest and a handful of folks at the gunwales keeping their eyes on the horizon. We won't get caught off-guard again."

They sailed south, keeping France on the horizon. Anyone who wasn't occupied with other tasks was put to work finishing the repairs. It was mostly cosmetic work and they were finished quickly. Cariad chose a piece of the gunwale that had been replaced. She elected that spot to signify the piece of the ship which had taken her eye and rested her hand on it. Part of the *Banshee* had pierced her flesh and left her permanently scarred. Her blood had soaked into the ship's deck, staining the wood. Even though her eye was patched and the bloody pieces of deck replaced, she still felt as if they'd been bound together.

"I'm part of you now," she whispered, running her hand over the smooth and freshly-painted wood. "And you're part of me. Let's keep each other safe, hm?"

The ship didn't respond. But Cariad walked away believing they had an understanding.

It was nearly twenty-four hours exactly after they'd spoken when Tis Common shouted a ship had been sighted on the horizon. The crew had spent the day preparing and practicing for what Fausta called "a little greeting," making sure the entire crew would know what was expected of them when they engaged the enemy.

Cariad felt the tension on deck rise as Ranzi climbed onto the rail, one hand clutching the rigging while the other brought a telescope up to her eye. Cariad could see the sails in the distance but only just. Everyone waited as Ranzi squinted. Then she lowered the scope and swung around on the rigging to face the quarterdeck.

"We found the bitch."

There was no shout of victory; the battle hadn't even begun yet. But Cariad felt a frisson of excitement pass through everyone around her. She turned to see Clio's eyes locked on her, and Cariad nodded that she was ready. She had Granny Wise's journal tucked into her belt and she removed it as she climbed the stairs to where Aravanis was steering them into an intercept course.

"You just need to be within eyesight, yes?" Harriet confirmed.

"And we need to be close enough to take advantage when it works," Clio added.

"*If* it works," Aravanis said.

Harriet said, "No pessimism! Not yet." She looked at Cariad.

"It will be your call. Clio is right. There's no point in doing this if she can just turn tail and run after you pulled your little gag."

"But not so close she can get a crippling shot in first," Clio said.

Cariad smiled through her sick feelings. "No pressure, then."

Clio patted Cariad on the shoulder.

They sailed closer, and the other ship came into sharper view. Coldness crept up Cariad's arms at the sight of it. The last time she'd seen this ship, she had been whole. This was the ship that had killed members of the crew, and it had forever changed her life. She tightened her jaw and opened the journal to the ritual she had shown the captains. Remaining silent was the hardest thing she had to do, but she had to make this count. The other ship's crew had spotted them. The ship was slowly, lazily turning like a fat cow preparing to swat a pestering fly.

Finally, finally, when she could almost see the reflection of the *Banshee* in the *Loyal Sea*'s windows, she determined they were close enough.

She opened the book.

It was a spoken spell, and she cleared her throat to make sure she wouldn't trip over the words. First she spoke the invocation to summon the power.

"Hear us and heed our cry, use your might to ease our suffering."

The sea around the *Banshee* began churning. Clio looked concerned, but Aravanis kept her eyes straight ahead on their target.

Cariad held the journal with one hand while she raised the other. Granny Wise had said it wasn't necessary to indicate the target, but it also helped if the spellcaster wanted to direct their efforts toward a particular field.

"Our mouths fill with ash and sand. No crops shall grow where we now stand." The next bit was the part she could alter for their specific needs. She had spent the past day trying to land on the proper wording. "Use your might, end their assault, and change their gunpowder into piles of salt."

A wave rose to their starboard and raced forward as if it had been caused by an undersea explosion. It slapped hard against the *Loyal Sea* and rocked it harder than Cariad would have thought possible. The wood creaked and the ship swung back and forth in place like it was drunk. It continued to turn until the *Banshee* was facing it broadside. Ronan's cannons pushed out through their peepholes, aimed directly at Clio's ship.

"Surrender your ship and all its cargo." Isobel Ronan's voice echoed from a bullhorn. "Refuse, and it will be lost at the bottom of this bay."

Aravanis said, "Shall I retrieve our horn to reply, Captain?"

"Not yet," Clio said.

The ships swayed silently, facing each other across a short stretch of water.

"Surrender means your people will live," Ronan said again. "You don't stand a chance aga~"

Silence fell again. Shouting could be heard on the *Loyal Sea*'s deck.

Clio calmly said, "Come about."

"Aye, coming about." Aravanis turned the wheel to starboard, slowly turning them so they would be alongside the *Loyal Sea* instead of facing it.

"Ready cannons."

"Ready cannons!" Fausta shouted.

From below, someone replied with a hearty, "Aye!" Cariad imagined she could feel the rumble through the wood as the heavy weapons were moved into position. On the other ship, through the open hatches their hopefully useless cannons protruded, she could hear angry shouting. Hopefully every grain or granule or whatever the fuck made up gunpowder on their ship had been transformed into useless piles of salt. Judging from the rising anger she heard, the spell had been successful.

"Let them hear you," Clio said, raising her voice just enough to be heard from the deck.

The sound started as a low hum near the quarterdeck, from those who had been close enough to hear the captain's order. It grew louder as it spread. No one stopped what they were doing, they just parted their lips and joined the chorus. Soon it was louder than the sound of the waves, louder than the shouts coming from the other ship.

It was the cry of the *Banshee*.

It was a low, keening howl that rose and fell as the people making it breathed in and out. Their voices all combined until it became the voice of the ship, a singular cry that you couldn't help but pay attention to. It seemed to ripple their sails and lift them higher in the water.

The cry slowly faded when Fausta gave the signal, and the

ensuing silence was almost crushing. Even the *Loyal Sea* had fallen quiet. The rigging of both ships creaked and strained above the quiet flap of the sails. Cariad looked back at Clio, holding her breath, certain everyone around her was doing the same.

Clio set her jaw, then bellow, "*Blow her out of the water!*"

The crew roared. The deck shuddered again, and the silence was shattered by the boom of a cannon. The *Loyal Sea* was already coming about, trying to flee, but the first volley of cannonballs tore into its side with a crash that Cariad felt in her chest. She knew people on that ship were being injured or maybe even dying, but she couldn't bring herself to care. They were brutal monsters who had earned every bit of suffering they were about to receive.

"Don't let her fucking run," she heard Clio say to Aravanis, handing the helm over to her.

Another round of cannon fire sounded, and more of their enemy's ship was broken away. Cariad could see into the gun deck where bloody sailors were scrambling to mount some kind of defense. Ranzi took position at one of their mounted guns and took aim at individual sailors. On the deck, *Loyal Sea* crewmen - much healthier and muscular than the starving rats that had crewed the ship the last time she saw them - fumbled and wrestled with their own weapons. Weapons that had been made useless by Cariad's spell, filled with sand.

The bastard ship was completely defanged.

It was running now, turned toward a nearby island thick with trees. Ranzi opened fire again, this time aiming for the sails. Bullets tore through the canvas, which eventually ripped and tore and began flapping in tatters, making it easy for the *Banshee* to close the distance between them.

Ronan's crew seemed to have given up on the long-range weapons and grabbed whatever else they had on hand, batons and swords and clubs, and prepared for boarding. A few intrepid souls actually hurled grappling hooks toward the *Banshee's* railing so they could swing across. Ranzi swung her gun around but paused before she fired again.

"Should we let them come?"

"No," Clio said, flat and cold.

"Aye-aye," Ranzi said, and shot the first few men who tried to make the jump. The bullets may not have killed them, but the fall to the water and subsequent abandonment would essentially be a death sentence.

It was a slaughter. Cariad watched bloody men fall off the other ship, saw bodies torn apart by bullets or cannonballs, and her stomach twisted. But this same crew had attacked them without provocation. They had thrown the opening punch, had drawn first blood. She knew that if Clio showed mercy here, the *Loyal Sea* would recover. They would go back to killing, thieving, and staging sneak attacks, and it would only be a matter of time before they targeted the *Banshee* again.

"We're going to kill them all, aren't we?"

She thought she'd spoken softly enough that no one would hear her, but Clio was closer than she'd realized. The captain came over and put a hand on Cariad's shoulder.

"If you don't want to be involved, you can go below. No one will hold it against you. It's ugly business. But–"

"I know," Cariad said. "I know what will happen if we allow them to keep sailing. I just have to convince myself it's the right thing to do. I broke their hands and now I'm watching them get pummeled. It feels wrong. It feels like an attack."

Clio nodded and moved her hand to the back of Cariad's head. "One of those men over there fired the cannon that took your eye. Remember that. And then think of the people who died in the same attack. Think of the people in Skala and the other places they hit who may go hungry because these bastards were greedy. They are not innocents."

Cariad met Clio's eye. "Neither are we."

Clio shook her head. "No one ever claimed we were." It was definitely Clio in charge; she saw no hint of Harriet in the gaze. "Are you going below?"

After a moment of thought, Cariad shook her head. "Someone needs to chronicle what happens here. It might as well be me."

"Agreed. Stay low. And if they board, be sure you're armed and ready to do some non-innocent things to keep them from taking our ship."

As she was speaking, the sky grew darker until the sun had been completely blotted out. Clio and Cariad looked up to see thick waves of storm clouds had developed directly above them.

"Dangers of battling a witch," Cariad said.

"You did warn us this might happen."

It was the main reason they had taken out the gun deck. Cariad warned that if Ronan had enough command over Granny Wise's magic to body-swap her entire crew, she could just change the salt back to gunpowder once she realized what happened. The cannons facing the *Banshee* were out of commission, so it seemed the witch was going with a different attack.

A sheet of rain swept across the ship from stern to bow, instantly soaking everyone who hadn't taken cover. The wind also picked up, nearly strong enough to knock people off their feet. Cariad grabbed a piece of the rigging and held on tightly as she watched everyone brace themselves against the surprise gale. Ranzi kept one hand on the gun as she crouched down, found a rope with her free hand, and used it to lash herself to the deck. She tied the knot tight around her waist and returned to firing at anyone attempting to board.

The distance between the two ships was growing rapidly. Cariad noticed this fact just as Clio shouted, "Do not let that bitch run, 'Vanis!"

"Aye!" Aravanis shouted over the crashing sound of rain.

It felt and sounded as if they had somehow steered the ship into a waterfall. It was raining so much that the water couldn't be bailed fast enough. Soon the deck was already submerged under several inches of water, which lapped at the ankles of the crew. The *Loyal Sea* continued its attempted retreat. Smoke rose from its starboard side, but Cariad couldn't make herself see that as a victory. If it somehow managed to escape, they could just rebuild. Hell, Ronan could just start over with a whole new ship by taking over their bodies.

Clio waded over to Cariad. "Anything else in that book of tricks that might help us out?"

Cariad's mind raced. "I don't think so…"

"It was written by the woman who did *this*!" She jabbed her finger into the sky. "There must be something."

"It seems there may have been some things she didn't bother writing down," Cariad snapped. Her hair was plastered to her head by the rain and hanging like a veil over her one good eye. She didn't dare release the rigging to swipe it away. "If I could turn the sea around her ship to ice, I would. If I could set the blasted thing on fire from here, it would be ashes in a heartbeat. It's a miracle the salt spell worked as well as it did. I'm sorry, Captain, but I'm all out of tricks."

"No, Miss Baillie, I'm sorry." Clio's voice was barely loud enough to be heard over the rain. She was squinting, so it was difficult to see the color of her eyes, but Cariad believed she was still speaking to the captain she knew and not Harriet. "You've done more than enough. Don't worry about keeping a record. Get below. Get somewhere safe."

"I can't~"

"Go! If anything happens to you, Estacia will blame me, and that woman has access to my food. I'm not risking it." She slapped Cariad on the arm. "You've given this ship your eye and a miracle. I won't have you sacrifice anything else for us. Go."

Cariad reluctantly let go of the ropes and turned, scanning for a doorway. Water cascaded down the steps, which meant she had to keep both hold of the handrail with a death grip to keep from being washed away. When she reached the bottom of the stairs, she saw people gathering water in buckets and hauling it into rooms where they could dump it out the windows.

With nothing else to do, she grabbed a spare bucket and hurried to join them.

The storm followed the *Banshee*, slowing its pursuit and giving the *Loyal Sea* enough room to pull ahead. Fortunately there was only one option for their battered enemy. It wouldn't be able to get to any ports for repairs. Their only option was the island they were currently limping toward. There was no point in running after someone when it was clear where they would end up. Ronan would have to run aground so they could effect repairs.

Clio had no intention of letting them get that far.

The storm abated as the distance between the two ships grew larger. The crew focused on bailing the water off the deck. Clio motioned for Ranzi and Fausta to join her on the quarterdeck with Aravanis.

"We have a decision to make," Clio said quietly. "We can destroy the ship and leave them stranded here, let nature take its course."

Harriet said, "Running the risk that someone will pass by and rescue them."

"Or we could finish the job," Clio continued. "I'm certain they will fight back, but make no mistake. If we go ashore, it will be with the intent of wiping out every single man and woman who sailed under Captain Ronan."

Ranzi said, "They made their decision already. Popped their brains out of their heads, shoved 'em in someone else's skull without permission. The body is already dead. Mind is, too. I have no problem stopping them from walking around."

Fausta shrugged. "Same. They tried to kill us."

"To be fair, they showed us a modicum of mercy. They let us scurry off to lick our wounds."

"Fear."

They all turned to look at Aravanis. When she saw them staring, she shrugged.

"It wasn't mercy," she explained. "They did it for fear. The same reason Ranzi was able to get so much information about them so quickly. They wanted ships to spread the word about them. They wanted crews to be afraid. They wanted the ports to know they were coming. When the *Banshee* dragged itself into Portsmouth with tattered sails, it wasn't an hour 'fore everyone knew who had done it. That's why they left us alive."

Fausta nodded slowly. "The woman has a point."

Ranzi said, "If you're asking for a vote, we have to do what we can to stop them. We've clearly made ourselves their enemies. They won't hesitate to end us, given the opportunity."

"Then it's agreed." Clio turned and looked at the ship. "Isobel Ronan and the *Loyal Sea* aren't leaving that island alive."

CHAPTER NINETEEN

THE CREW of the *Loyal Sea* crowded on the beach and watched the *Banshee*'s approach. Some of them were still trying to make their guns work, their angry curses sweeping across the water. Eventually they threw the useless weapons down and armed themselves with clubs and swords, daggers, cudgels, anything that could do some damage at close quarters.

Clio, meanwhile, had their own armory emptied out. It felt a little ruthless to indulge in such an unbalanced fight, but she couldn't bring herself to pity the bastards of Isobel Ronan's ship. She no longer cared how they might have suffered under John Ronan's cruelty. They stopped being victims when they decided their lives were worth more than the Barbary pirates, when they let the cruelty they'd endured make them cruel in return. They'd killed an entire crew of men they'd considered 'less than' so they could be stronger.

Fausta approached the captain as they closed in on the shore. "The crew is prepared, captain. How do you want to play this?"

If they took the *Banshee* in close enough to disembark on foot, that would give the *Loyal Sea* men a chance to board. She trusted her crew would be able to fight them off, but she didn't want to give them the chance to cause any damage to her shiny new ship. But the longboat only carried seven people, at most, and that was a recipe for disaster. One boat, seven people, and a whole ship worth of enemies waiting for them on the beach.

She chewed her lip as she considered her options. "Prepare the launch," she said. "Take Aravanis and Ranzi and three volunteers. Come at them from the north..." She held her arm out, curving her hand to indicate the path. "We'll cut to the south and clear them out a bit with the guns. We might hit a couple, force the others to take cover in the trees."

Fausta nodded. "Aravanis will probably be willing to stand in the bow and pick them off with a rifle as we make our approach."

Clio nodded. "That plan works for me."

"And for me, captain." Fausta left to gather her crew.

Clio unclipped the spyglass from her belt and brought it up to her eye, scanning the people on the beach. None of them looked like Isobel Ronan. She didn't know if that meant she had stayed on the ship, if she was in the trees somewhere, or if she had taken the opportunity to swap to a new body.

She didn't know what she would do if she'd gone to that length. She wanted to take her revenge on Isobel, the woman who had stranded her, the woman who had nearly destroyed the *Banshee* and ruined the lives of her crew. It wouldn't be as satisfying, or offer as much closure, if she was in the body of a stranger.

"She didn't change," Harriet said, listening in on her thoughts.

Clio lowered the spyglass. "You sound very confident about that."

"She wanted power and respect. She got it. She's not going to take the chance someone else gets the credit. She wants people to fear the name Isobel Ronan. She'll be in her own body, and she'll be waiting when we get to the island."

"When *we* get to the island..."

Clio chewed her bottom lip, then turned and scanned the crew for Fausta. She went to where she was loading her pockets with extra ammunition.

"I'm coming with you."

"With all due respect, Captain, it's best for you to–"

"The bitch left me on an island to die," Clio said.

Fausta looked up and met Clio's gaze. She saw something she recognized there, a fire and determination, and she nodded.

"Load up. We'll be happy to have you at our side."

Clio nodded and clapped her on the shoulder as she went to arm herself.

The crew of the *Loyal Sea* didn't linger on the beach when it became clear that a fight was coming. Clio heard a man shouting orders to the others and watched them scatter, taking cover in the trees. They might not have projectile weapons, but they could do plenty of damage by throwing rocks or planning an ambush. Clio had warned everyone to keep their eyes open and their heads on a swivel. They might have superior weaponry, but Ronan's crew had the advantage of setting up the field of battle.

Aravanis did indeed take position in the bow with a rifle but, by the time they were within firing range, the beach had been cleared of potential targets. Clio could still hear them shouting to each other in the wooded area. She spotted one man scurrying up a tree and pointed him out to Ranzi. Ranzi nodded; she'd already anticipated attacks from above.

Clio twisted to look at their three volunteers. Two of them were male, Robert and Hoyle, but the third had surprised her. Harriet, on the other hand, thought it was inevitable.

Cariad sensed the captain looking at her and met her gaze. She'd gotten her spot by claiming she needed to document the attack. Clio and Harriet both knew that her reasons for going along went deeper than that, and those reasons were why she had asked for a pistol. She'd claimed it was for protection, but she hadn't even bothered to conceal the truth in her tone. She wanted revenge, a literal eye for her eye. Clio wasn't ordinarily one to endorse revenge but, at the moment, she thought it was a necessary attitude to take into the battle. She currently considered Cariad Baillie the deadliest member of her crew by a wide margin.

When they hit land, Aravanis leapt from the launch and dropped to one knee, scanning the tree line with her rifle while the others joined her. Whispers came from the darkness, and it was difficult to tell if the movement of leaves and branches was due to wind or someone shifting position. Clio knelt beside Aravanis and rested a hand on her shoulder.

"You have the beach, 'Vanis."

"I shall hold," Aravanis said, no hint of hesitation in her voice.

"Good woman." Clio turned and motioned Fausta and Hoyle to come with her. She signaled for Ranzi, Cariad, and Robert to attack the right side of the beach. Ranzi nodded and led the way. Clio rose and charged for the trees.

Clio spotted the first volley, a large gray stone, with more than enough time to dodge out of the way so it landed with a dull thud in the sand. More stones came, but the attack was pathetic enough that the *Banshee* crew would have had to be blindfolded for it to have any hope of success. Throwing the stones only served to give Clio somewhere to aim. She brought up her pistol and pinpointed where the stones seemed to be coming from and fired. Fausta and Hoyle fired in the same spot, and they were rewarded with a shout of pain.

At the tree line, they stopped to make sure the man had been dispatched. He was lying flat on his back in a pile of fallen leaves which had been splattered with his blood. The wound was high in his right shoulder and rendered that arm useless. He glared up at Clio with rage, and she shrugged indifferently to his anger.

"It must be terribly frustrating to get a brand-new body just to have it ruined immediately," Harriet said, and Clio laughed. She must have sounded mad, like she was laughing at her own joke, but she didn't care. She continued on, not bothering to secure the injured stone thrower. Isobel would have only left him behind to cover their retreat if he was expendable. She would save her worry for whoever was waiting further down the trail.

She heard more gunfire from the right and assumed Ranzi's squad had also engaged their enemy. She wished she had told Ranzi to keep Isobel for her. She wanted to be the one who took the bitch out. But she was also glad she hadn't said anything. If Ranzi got a clear shot, she should take it. The only thing Clio could do was hope she'd chosen the correct path and Isobel was somewhere up ahead.

The trees began to spread out as the ground sloped steadily upward. Clio briefly thought that Isobel was making a huge tactical error, retreating uphill and quickly losing cover, but she realized she was the one potentially running blind. She held up a hand top stop the rest of her group and crouched down behind a tree, her shoulder against the bark as she considered the possibilities.

"What are you thinking?" Fausta asked.

It was Harriet who answered. "Assuming it's Isobel Ronan we're pursuing, she's too clever to flee like this. It's highly likely to be an ambush."

"She'll have the high ground soon enough," Clio agreed. "If

there's a clearing up ahead, she'll have the advantage of seeing us coming. We're making enough noise, she'd know exactly where to expect us to appear. She'll be waiting."

Fausta grimaced. "So how do we use that against her?"

Hoyle held up his dagger. "We make her flinch."

He pushed between them and was off at a full run before either could stop him. Clio swore under her breath and started to pursue, but Fausta grabbed her arm.

"He's an idiot, but he's not wrong. Isobel will most likely attack as soon as she sees him, and then her element of surprise will be gone. We just have to follow him quietly, cautiously, and we'll know where the ambush is and what she's planning. If he gets killed, it's his own fault for thinking he's in charge."

Harriet agreed with Fausta, but Clio still felt horrible for letting a member of her crew do something so foolish. But it was his choice. He hadn't given her a chance to say no, so Fausta was right. Anything that happened to him would be his doing. She rose and hurried after Hoyle in a crouched position with Fausta behind her doing the same.

Hoyle used his sword to cut through branches, shouting with every slice, crashing through underbrush as if he expected every leaf to contain an enemy. As Clio had predicted, the coverage soon ended and he emerged into a wide clearing. He had barely made it three steps before an arrow slammed into his chest with enough force that it threw him backward.

Clio and Fausta immediately dropped lower. Fausta craned her neck up. She looked at Hoyle, then dipped her chin, squinting beyond him. Clio knew exactly what she was doing: using the angle of the arrow to determine where it had come from.

"I know where they are," she said.

"Take them out," Clio said.

Fausta brought her gun up and fired. She kept firing as she broke cover, and Clio heard someone shout in pain. Clio broke cover as well and joined Fausta in the clearing. She fired where Fausta was aiming. The archer had already been taken out, but Isobel was reaching to recover his weapon and quiver. Fausta ricocheted a bullet off the ground near the fallen man's outstretched hand, which made Isobel recoil to avoid being hit by the next shot. She was already on her knees and apparently decided it wasn't worth the effort to scramble up to get to her feet.

"I think it's fair to say you've been bested here, Captain

Ronan," Clio said as she approached. "Surrender now and we won't feel the need to put any holes in you."

Isobel sneered at her. "Compassion? Now? After you destroyed my ship?"

"Retribution can be cruel," Clio said. "People don't have to be. I'd really prefer not to kill you here, but if you test me..."

Isobel looked at the two men with her, then looked at Fausta. Something in the first mate's face told her that fighting would be useless. She relaxed her shoulders and, with a sigh, raised both hands.

"I'm not sure what you intend for the next step," Isobel said. "I'll be put in a cell while the authorities attempt to unravel exactly what crimes I've committed. It won't be an easy job, because half the justices won't believe the story is possible. Souls jumping from one body to another? It's sorcery! Madness! And while they argue about whether I'm a criminal or a lunatic, I'll be working out a way to escape. I'll find another ship, another crew, and continue to earn my reputation."

Fausta scoffed. "Some reputation. Your ship was destroyed by the first enemy you picked a fight with. Your hand-picked crew could barely hold their own in a fight. Those who survived, anyway."

An idea sparked in Clio's mind. She passed it to Harriet, who examined it and agreed with her. She found it odd to have a completely silent interaction like that, but she was grateful for the opportunity it gave her to scheme. She looked at Isobel and waited until the other woman met her gaze.

"The problem is that you started from scratch. You might have been more successful if you'd taken over your husband's body. Used his reputation to build your own. Your downfall was caused by your ego, your vanity. Continuing as Isobel Ronan might only bring mockery and humiliation."

Fausta moved closer. "Captain...?"

Clio waved her off. "You're a formidable foe, Captain Ronan. I've never gone up against anyone like you before. If we chose to join forces, we would be unstoppable. It would certainly be more productive than just punching at each other whenever our paths cross."

Isobel narrowed her eyes. "I suppose that's true."

Fausta looked between the two of them. "Captain," she said again, this time with much more concern in her voice. "Are you feeling... well?"

"At the moment we're at a stalemate, Miss Gittens," Clio said, not taking her eyes off Isobel. "This benefits both of us. We could be the strongest ship in the sea. I have nearly a decade of reputation. She wouldn't have to waste time making a name. All that respect, there for the taking, with none of the work."

Isobel said, "If we do this, the witch will remain in my body..."

Clio shrugged. "Let her have it. She'll know better than to cross us. Besides, I've got a witch of my own. A member of my crew has spent a lot of time reading Granny Wise's journals, and she has the benefit of youth on her side. She knows all about this body swapping business. She's been babbling about primaries and ether and I've no idea what else. She could keep the old bat in her place. And she's probably the weakest member of my crew. Look at Fausta here. Ranzi. Aravanis and Delfina. Can you honestly say your men hold a candle to my women?"

Isobel eyed the men she had surrendered with. Finally she rose to her feet and approached Clio.

"Let's do it."

Clio grinned and held out her hand. Isobel clasped her forearm and squeezed tight. Clio pulled her closer and stared into the other captain's eyes. She saw something flicker behind the irises and hoped it was Granny Wise drifting closer to the surface.

"Do you know the words required?"

"I do."

"Hold them in your mind," Clio said. "Concentrate on your destination."

The last thing they needed was a 'hiccup,' as Cariad called it, and Clio decided there was one surefire thing she could do.

She kissed Isobel hard, on the lips, the contact as violent as a punch.

Her hand tightened on Isobel's arm to keep her from pulling away. Isobel struggled, and Clio focused her thoughts on Harriet. She could feel Harriet doing the same for her. Together they formed a wall. And when a darkness pressed against them, they created a solid wall to push back against it. Isobel's body jerked and twitched. The darkness pressed harder. Clio tightened her grip. She put her other hand on the back of Isobel's head and held her still, continuing the kiss as the dark wave of Isobel Ronan's consciousness pressed against the breakwater of Clio and Harriet's defenses.

Just when Clio's strength began to wane, she felt something give. The ocean of Isobel Ronan began to disperse and scatter. It twisted around itself in a panicked scatter until, at last, it was swept away like it had been caught in a gust of wind. Cariad said when two souls shared the same body, one potential outcome was the intruder being forced out "into the ether." The second soul merely needed to be drawn out, and then the door had to be closed behind it.

Clio broke the kiss and took a step back.

"Harriet~" Clio gasped at the same time Harriet tried to say, "Are you okay?"

They were still holding tight to Isobel Ronan's arm, but the other woman had collapsed to her knees. She looked like a marionette whose puppeteer had abandoned it. Clio gently lowered the woman to the ground and tried to find signs that her gambit had failed.

Isobel's eyes were open but scanned the sky as if she expected something to be written on the clouds. Finally she blinked once, twice, and then she focused on Clio's face. She smiled.

"That was very risky." Her voice was unmistakably different, more world-weary than it had been moments ago.

"But worth the effort...?" Clio asked hopefully.

"She's gone," Granny Wise confirmed.

Clio released a heavy sigh, full of relief. "Thank goodness for that."

"Clever to get my attention by mentioning the primary," Granny Wise said. "It let me know I should be prepared to block her from slipping back inside."

"I wasn't sure that was an option. But I wanted to be sure you knew what I was doing."

"You did wonderfully." She grunted as she sat up. "You should probably restrain me until you're absolutely certain who you're dealing with. Just as a precaution."

Fausta said, "With all due respect, how are we supposed to determine that? You could be Isobel Ronan trying to trick us."

"Exactly why I suggested tying me up. Captain Landau, you mentioned a member of your crew had been studying my books. Was that true?"

"Indeed. Cariad Baillie."

Granny Wise smiled. It was a kinder, more beatific smile than Isobel Ronan had likely ever produced.

"I would very much like to meet Miss Baillie."

Cariad approached the woman she knew as Isobel Ronan, not entirely convinced the evil captain was gone despite Clio's assurances. The woman's hands were still bound behind her back, her head bowed, and she was kneeling in the sand. When she looked up, Cariad was surprised to see how soft her eyes were. She smiled and there seemed to be genuine kindness in the expression. Cariad stopped a few feet away from her.

"Miss Baillie. Your captain speaks highly of you, dear." Isobel's voice was rougher than Cariad expected, like stones tapping against each other. It was how she knew that she was listening to Granny Wise. "Very well done, young lady. I thought it would take someone years to figure it out. You did some phenomenal work. I laughed and laughed when they realized what you'd done to the gunpowder." She chuckled and shook her head. "Oh, Isobel hated hearing that sound in her head, I can tell you that. She kept asking me how to undo it, and I used all my strength to keep her from unlocking that spell."

Cariad managed a weak smile. "I'm glad to know I caused her some frustration."

"She deserved all she got." Granny Wise looked at the row of captured *Loyal Sea* sailors. "I understand you're here to keep me in check, just in case I'm lying or trying to trick you all. I don't care what spell of mine you plucked out of the journal, it won't be quick enough. If anyone here thinks I'm doing something untoward, I suggest that one~" She nodded at Ranzi. "~use her sword and just take my head off at the neck."

Ranzi put her hand on the hilt of her weapon. "I'd be fine with that."

Granny Wise pressed her lips together and nodded. "I've lived four hundred years. I've taken the bodies of people who came to me with, hum... terrible goals. People who wanted to use my power to destroy others, to rule, for pain and suffering. Many of them have been strong-willed. None of them have been able to wrestle control away from me like Ronan did. Maybe it's a sign that my time is done. Either way, whichever way, I only want to help. These men did awful things. I would be more than happy to put them in stones for you."

Cariad opened the pouch on her belt. She had gathered stones on her walk from the ship. They were simple, ugly stones, full of jagged edges and unremarkable in every way. She held them out for Granny Wise to inspect, and the old witch nodded her head.

"Good, very good. No wonder you were able to use my spells. You've got a knack." She smiled up at Cariad. "Keep my book, love. And the next time you visit Islas Baleares, even if I'm not with you, I'll make sure you're able to find the others I have hidden. I want you to have them. I think you'll do great things with them."

"You'll make sure...?" Cariad frowned. "How?"

Granny Wise laughed. "I have ways, child. No one could find me if I didn't want them to. And no one will ever find those books unless you're the one looking."

Cariad didn't know how to respond to that. "Thank you."

Clio nodded to Fausta. "Untie her hands."

Granny Wise leaned forward so she could be freed. Once the ropes were gone, she held out her hands for the stones.

"Come with me, Miss Baillie, and I'll show you how this works. In case it ever comes up again."

Cariad was still skeptical, but she went.

Clio watched the first two transfers, twitching when the first man slumped to the ground after the soul occupying him was removed. The second struggled but still went down just as easily. When Granny Wise moved on to the third, Clio suddenly found herself turning away and walking into the forest. She wrapped her arms around herself, head down to watch her feet move of their own volition.

"Any idea where we're headed?" she finally asked.

"I want to see the ocean one final time." Harriet's voice was weak.

Clio said, "We don't have to do this."

"We do." Harriet sighed. "Even if I just... faded away, it wouldn't be fair to you. It would change who you are as a person."

"And I would be *fine* with that."

"I wouldn't be. I don't want to change you."

Clio sighed. "I miss you, Harriet."

"I know. But this isn't a life. Jumping from one body to another. And living like this is no real answer. I can't see you. I can't hold you in my arms. I can't kiss you goodbye."

They emerged from the trees into a clearing. They were on a cliff that looked down over the harbor where the *Banshee* and the remains of the *Loyal Sea* swayed peacefully on the tide.

"It's best to see this for what it is. A visitation. So we can say goodbye. So I can see that my trust in you was worthwhile. So I can apologize for keeping the truth of your identity from you for so long."

"And a gift," Clio added. "Knowing that we... That something exists after death. Another place, another existence. It's possible. You're proof of that. I just have to be patient. I'll see you again."

"It will be worth the wait," Harriet said quietly. She hugged herself. "The harder we hold onto this moment, the more it will slip away. The more time we'll waste. So let's simply enjoy the view."

"Okay, Harriet."

A tear rolled down their cheek. Clio didn't know if it was hers or Harriet's, but it probably didn't matter.

By the end there were plenty of tears for them to share.

CHAPTER TWENTY

IT ONLY took a half hour for Granny Wise to imprison the crew of the *Loyal Sea*. None of the men survived; their original souls had been completely eradicated so the replacements could have complete control. Clio asked for volunteers to bury the bodies and was heartened when many of her crew immediately picked up spades and shovels and got to work. Cariad took the stones with the captive souls and promised Granny Wise she would find somewhere to keep them. Granny Wise watched her go, then turned to Clio. She approached slowly, hands out.

"I take it you two are ready...?"

Harriet said, "I'm ready. It's nearly sunset. That feels appropriate." She cleared her throat and gestured behind her. "There's a clearing just through there. It overlooks the sea. I thought that might be a good place for it."

"I agree. It's always nice to do it somewhere beautiful." She held up a piece of sea glass. It was dark purple at its wide base, slowly turning more indigo and blue as it narrowed. "I saved this one for you. I thought it would be a nice place for a good soul."

Harriet smiled sadly. "It's gorgeous. But... do I have to go into a stone?"

Granny Wise tilted her head one way in order to look at Clio.

"Well... if you wish to ever be awakened again..." She tilted her head another way, looked at Harriet. Understanding passed between them. She shook her head slowly, giving Harriet a compassionate smile. "No. You don't have to go into the stone. I can release you."

"Then that's what I want. Clio, I'm sorry, but~"

"No," Clio spoke over her. "I understand. The stone is a prison. You deserve to be free. I won't keep you from whatever comes next. You've earned that peace."

"Thank you," Harriet whispered.

Granny Wise said, "You're certain?"

"Positive. Let's go."

They started toward the clearing, but stopped at the sound of someone shouting Clio's name. They waited and watched until Delfina appeared. She was out of breath, her eyes desperate. She saw the glass stone in Granny Wise's hand, then looked at Clio in panic.

"You haven't done it yet, have you?"

"No," Clio said. "We were just about to."

Delfina sighed, relieved. "Good. Put Harriet in me."

Harriet shook her head. "Absolutely not. I appreciate the offer, Delfina, but I will not be a passenger in~"

"Not permanently," Delfina said. "For the goodbye. You can't say goodbye like this. And as someone who has loved you both, I would be honored if I could help you have a proper farewell."

Granny Wise raised her eyebrows and shrugged. "I'm willing."

Harriet smiled, tears in her eyes. "Well... I suppose one more detour couldn't hurt."

"Not when it's a noble cause," Granny Wise agreed. "Come along. I'll do it at the location."

They walked through the trees. Clio looked back at the witch. "I noticed you didn't do a, ah... With every other..." She tried to think of what she wanted to say. "There was an element of the receptacle being open to the new arrival. Harriet's first host was taken mid-orgasm."

"Oh my!" Granny Wise laughed. "That must have been quite a shock."

Harriet smiled with Clio's lips. "It was peculiar, to say the least..."

"The second involved a gun being fired next to my head. You didn't do any of that with the *Loyal Sea* crew. Will it be required here?"

"No, no," Granny Wise said. "That's more of a... hm... well, this is a poor explanation. But when you are learning to cook a meal, you have the recipe written down next to you, and you follow every single instruction to the letter. But once you've made the meal enough times, ah, then you know the way, then you can begin to improvise and put your own mark on things. Miss Baillie was good, she's very good, but the brain hiccough isn't strictly necessary if one knows what she's doing. And I have been doing this for a very, very long time."

Clio sighed. "I suppose that's a good thing."

They arrived at the clearing. As predicted, the sun was nearly touching the horizon.

Clio turned to Delfina. "Thank you for this."

"It's an honor," Delfina said.

Granny Wise said, "Face one another, please."

They did, and the witch placed her hand on the back of Clio's head. Delfina's hair was longer and untied, so she had to reach underneath to place her fingertips on the base of her skull. She closed her eyes and concentrated. She clicked her tongue against her teeth and shook her head.

"Got quite comfortable in there, didn't you?"

"Sorry," Harriet said.

"Hmm. It isn't as if you had a mentor to tell you it was a bad idea. But it's not irreversible, not yet. It might be a little rougher than I expected, but I can still do it."

"Rougher as in... pain?" Delfina asked.

"No pain," Granny Wise promised, her eyes still closed. "Rough seas. That's all." She hummed a series of low notes.

Clio felt a sharp jab at the back of her skull, like one of the witch's fingers had just poked her with its nail. Before she could even register the pain, it twisted and pulled. She gasped and recoiled, but the hand was gripping her neck too tightly. The pain was brief enough that it had already passed by the time she opened her eyes.

Despite the fact they were basically the same age, Delfina's hair had retained its full black color. Now, however, the ends were a solid gray. Her eyes were closed and she breathed in deeply before opening them. She focused on Clio and a calm, serene smile spread across her face.

"There you are," Harriet said.

Granny Wise dropped her hands and took a step back. "I'll

give you ladies a moment."

"Thank you."

Clio watched her go, then looked down at her arm. The tattoo she'd gotten accustomed to seeing had vanished. Harriet saw her looking and rolled up Delfina's sleeve. The tattoo had appeared on her skin, just above her elbow. She brushed it with her thumb as if she expected the ink to smear.

"Remarkable."

"Very much so." Clio winced and touched her temple. "It feels so odd now. I got used to hearing you in there. Now it feels... it's empty. Just me knocking around."

Harriet said, "It feels odd here, too. I got used to your body. Delfina's is..." She tilted her head to the side and laughed. "No, no, it is. It's very nice, Delf. You know how much I enjoyed it when we were together. But being inside you is much different than..." She laughed again. "Hush. Let me say goodbye to my wife. Saucy minx."

Clio shook her head. "I forgot the two of you could be so..."

"Flirtatious?"

"Intolerable," Clio corrected with a smile. She cupped Harriet's cheek and brushed her thumb over the skin. "The past few weeks have been a gift I never could have hoped for. I never realized how much it hurt, knowing I didn't have the opportunity to say goodbye to you. When we retrieved your..." She stopped herself before she said the word. "I said goodbye then. But it didn't give me the closure I needed. So I will say it now.

"Goodbye, Harriet. Thank you for giving me a life I treasure. You gave me a name, a purpose. You made me into someone I could be proud of. I don't blame you for burying Alice Malyns. She died at your hand, and good riddance to her. I am and shall always be Clio Landau, and that is because you saved me. Thank you. And thank you for loving me."

Harriet sighed and looked down, tears filling her eyes. "I expected it to hurt, seeing how much you had flourished without me. But I'm so proud. Seeing you in command, seeing the respect the crew has for you. You're a better captain than me. And you're lucky that I love you too much to be pissed off about that."

Clio laughed and brushed away one of Harriet's tears.

"But I want you to be happy. One of the benefits of being in Delfina's head is knowing that the two of you have found comfort with each other. That makes me happy. You are two people I love more than anyone else in this world. And if I can't be with you, you deserve each other. Stop pretending it isn't something more. Give in to it. Love each other. Be with each other."

It was Clio's turn to start crying.

"I'll always be part of you, Clio. Now more than ever. I wanted to share my life with you and now I have done that in ways we never could have dreamed possible. I'm sure there were a few little specks and spots of my soul that Granny Wise didn't get. Don't be afraid to use them to guide you when you're uncertain. Don't worry about me. I'm excited to see what happens next. Wherever I end up, I'll wait for you there."

"I can't wait to see you."

"Take your time. You have a long life to live yet. And you are worth waiting for." She bent down and, just before her lips met Clio's, she said, "I love you, Clio Landau."

"I love you too, Harriet Landau. Goodbye."

"Goodbye."

They kissed. The sun set.

Delfina moaned softly, tensed, and then stepped closer to Clio. She put her arms around the captain's waist, and Clio put her hands in the small of Delfina's back to keep her close. Their kiss deepened and became more passionate, both women leaning into each other until finally Delfina turned her head and brushed her lips across Clio's cheek.

"You need to know~"

"I know." Clio kissed Delfina's cheek. "I felt her go. I know."

Delfina rested her head on Clio's shoulder.

Clio knew that Granny Wise still lurked somewhere nearby, trying not to disturb their moment. And she knew that the darker it got, the more treacherous it would be getting through the wooded area back to the beach. But at the moment she couldn't bring herself to care. She wanted to stay there until Harriet was really, truly gone.

She'd abandoned her wife to die alone once before. She wasn't going to make the same mistake a second time.

EPILOGUE

CARIAD WAS surprised to find that it seemed wrong to loot the *Loyal Sea*. There was no reason not to. The crew was dead, the ship was unsalvageable, and it seemed only right that the money spent to repair the *Banshee* was repaid by those who had caused the damage. But regardless of how logical it was, it made her feel like a vulture to dig through the possessions left behind by the vanquished crew. She remained in the quarters, writing down a chronicle of the fight that had ended Isobel Ronan and her singular crew.

When the ship had been thoroughly picked clean, the *Banshee* set sail and left the *Loyal Sea*'s carcass where it had run aground. Cariad had gone up on deck to observe its shattered hull and limp sails one final time as they returned to the sea, their destination somewhere in the Mediterranean. They were taking Granny Wise back to Baleares where she would consider her next steps.

"My grip on a new body has never been that weak," she explained when she came aboard the *Banshee*. "Maybe Isobel was stronger than everyone else I've swapped bodies with, though I doubt that very much. And maybe even souls have limitations in how long they can stick around. I'd like to have more of a choice in how and when my road ends."

Cariad had gone to her cabin when they got back to the ship, and Cariad hadn't seen her in the three days they'd been sailing. Delfina had gone to check on her a few times but she'd given no reports or updates to the crew. Those who were in command knew she was grieving, and everyone seemed willing to give her as much time as she needed.

On the fourth day of their journey, Cariad found Granny Wise at the railing. She was cradling something in her hand. When Cariad got closer, she saw it was the stones in which the *Loyal Sea* crew had been confined. The witch smiled at her as she approached.

"I'm just trying to decide what to do with these." She juggled the stones in her palm. She plucked one up at random and held it over the side. "Burial at sea, perhaps? Many sailors whose lives I experienced believed that was the ultimate goal. And it wouldn't be as if I was murdering them. And yet... they could live again, if I so decided."

"But they were murderers," Cariad reminded her. "Cruel and violent. They would have met an untimely end regardless of what happened on that island. Why would you use your gift to bring them back? Why would you leave them around so someone else could summon them?"

Granny Wise nodded. "You have a point. It's the choice, you see. Bring them back, dump them in the ocean. Either way, I am deciding if these men live or die. That is a terrible power for one person to have. I'm finding myself very conflicted. If I elect to keep the stones, and they fell into the hands of another Isobel Ronan, I would be responsible for whatever horrors they might commit."

Cariad said, "I'm not sure I agree with that. Their actions would be their own. You wouldn't be culpable for what someone did just because you spared their life. Fausta saved my life when I lost my eye. She isn't responsible for anything I might do in the future."

"Be that as it may," Granny Wise said, "I think this entire endeavor has proven that life needs to have an ending. Harriet Landau knew that, despite how hard it was to say goodbye. She left because it was the right thing to do."

After a long moment of contemplation, Granny Wise sighed and held her hand out over the railing. She slowly turned her wrist and let the stones roll and tumble over themselves until they splashed far below in the water.

"They had a life, the same life everyone else gets," Granny Wise said. "And they made their choice in how to live it."

"I agree."

Granny Wise wiped off her hands as if the stones had left residue. "As for me... I was given more life than anyone could dream of. And I used it hiding. Living through others. Now I have this young, strong body, I think I should actually experience the world for myself. See what trouble I can get into, rather than just standing outside looking in. It's a bit terrifying, though. Knowing that if it ends, I'm gone forever."

Cariad nodded. "Terrifying, sure. But it makes everything a little sweeter. More precious."

"I can't wait to see what's out there."

"Whatever you find," Cariad said, "I promise it will be worth the danger."

Granny Wise looked at her. "You're saying that...?"

Cariad touched her eyepatch. She could have been on the mainland, safe, with both eyes intact. In some dark office, arguing with an editor about what was worth printing in the newspaper. She could spend her nights alone reading by lantern. She could have a nice, quiet life of taverns and sitting by the harbor and writing quaint stories of island life that no one bothered to read.

"Yes," she said. "I'm saying that. And I absolutely believe that. Nothing lost, nothing won. Living. Not surviving."

Granny Wise smiled at her. "I like how you think, Miss Baillie."

Cariad shrugged. "We all make our choices. No matter what happens, it's better to choose a life than settling into one."

"Maybe you're the one they should call 'wise,' young lady."

Cariad laughed and patted the witch's shoulder, leaving her to her musings. She had found a life she adored, stumbling into it with no plan or destination in mind. She'd never expected to find purpose on a pirate ship. Hiring the *Banshee* had been a means to an end. But when she tried to leave after the mission was over, she found herself longing for a return. It was more than just a desire to be with Estacia again, although that was a big part of what drew her back to the harbor.

She spotted Fausta and crossed the deck to where she was working. The first mate glanced up at her approach and went back to what she was doing. When Cariad stopped, Fausta looked up again.

"Do you need something, Miss Baillie?"

"It took me a long time to realize something. I had a lot of things on my mind when I woke up with one eye. But eventually I did remember that when the *Loyal Sea* attacked us, when I was hurt, I was holding my journal. It seemed odd that it had somehow found its way back to my cabin after everything. I couldn't imagine I'd been able to hold onto it while I was unconscious. You didn't just save my life. You saved my journal. My work."

Fausta kept her head down. "I know how important that thing is to you. Figured you'd be a pain in the ass if I just left it."

Cariad smiled. "Very much so."

She walked on, knowing that a full expression of gratitude would only make Fausta uncomfortable. But maybe she could convince Estacia to make her something nice for dinner.

Thinking of Estacia made her smile, and she quickened her pace. A pirate ship, a chef with a killer smile, a journal full of adventures with plenty of space more, and books of magic that would, possibly, give her unearthly powers to help keep the ship and its crew safe.

It wasn't the life she had expected, but it certainly wasn't a life she was just settling for. She had chosen this life, and she was excited to see what it had in store next.

Six days after they left the *Loyal Sea*, the *Banshee* sailed through the Strait of Gibraltar. Their return to the Mediterranean was marked by the reemergence of Clio Landau from the exile in her cabin. Conversation on the deck stopped when she first appeared. Her shirt was laundered and seemed to glow in the sunlight, its high collar brushing her jaw and the sleeves just long enough that only her fingers were visible poking past the cuffs. She wore black trousers with a red line up the outer thigh and a belt with a large gold buckle.

She ignored the staring as she ascended to the quarterdeck. Ranzi was at the helm and dutifully took a step back so Clio could take her place steering. Clio nodded her thanks as she wrapped her fingers around the handles of the wheel. She squinted into the sky, then looked ahead at the open sea.

"It's good to see you again, Captain," Ranzi said.

Clio nodded slowly. "It's good to be back. It was rough seas for a bit." She flexed her fingers and tightened her grip. "But I knew I could pass through it. In time." She turned her head so she could see Ranzi and Aravanis in her periphery. "It was good knowing I had a crew I could count on to pick up the slack while I grieved."

"We were prepared to give you as much time as you needed."

"It was greatly appreciated, I assure you. What's our heading?"

"Back to Baleares," Ranzi said. "We can take Granny Wise home, check on Santiago. And there are bound to be jobs on offer, plenty of opportunities to find something normal for the next few weeks."

"Normal would be nice," Clio agreed. "So Baleares it is."

Ranzi nodded. "Aye-aye, Captain."

Clio smiled and lifted her chin, eyes on the horizon, both hands firmly on the wheel.

To Baleares.

And whatever lay beyond it.

ABOUT THE AUTHOR

Geonn Cannon is the author of over sixty novels, including the Riley Parra series which was adapted into an Emmy-nominated webseries by Tello Films. His novel *Can You Hear Me* was adapted into *Static Space*, an award-winning short film. He's also written two tie-in novels for the television series *Stargate SG-1*. He was the first male author to win a Golden Crown Literary Society Award for his novel *Gemini*, and he won a second for *Dogs of War*.